STARING AT HIS OWN GRAVE

The area was littered with cigar butts and whiskey bottles. From the boot imprints, he decided that seven to eight men made up the gang, two of them quite large.

A cross had been made from two pieces of tree limb and tamped into the ground. Rocks and fresh soil were heaped in front of the cross, enough to signify that a man's grave might lay there.

At first Windham believed the Jayhawkers had buried one of their number. Upon close inspection, though, he saw that the cross had been left for him.

Carved in the wood were the words: FRANK WIND-HAM.

Windham pulled the cross from the ground and studied it, wondering who would have gone to such trouble. It had to be someone who hated him a great deal.

That could mean a lot of people.

JAYHAWKER CROSSING

JACK STANFORD

A TOM DOHERTY ASSOCIATES BOOK
NEW YORK

This is a work of fiction. All the characters and events portrayed in this book are fictitious, and any resemblance to real people or events is purely coincidental.

JAYHAWKER CROSSING

Cover art by Royo

A Tor Book
Published by Tom Doherty Associates, Inc.
175 Fifth Avenue
New York, N.Y. 10010

Tor® is a registered trademark of Tom Doherty Associates, Inc.

ISBN: 0-812-53399-2

First edition: September 1994

Printed in the United States of America

0 9 8 7 6 5 4 3 2 1

To the memory of Jack LeMond

One

THUNDERHEADS ROLLED over the Cimarron, dropping jagged streaks of light down from the late evening sky. Three thousand longhorn steers milled restlessly across an open grassy plain while drovers circled them, singing loudly over a gusty wind.

Frank Windham sat near the chuck-wagon fire, sipping thick coffee, watching the developing storm. He rubbed his right leg, just above the ankle, where a Confederate bullet had chipped out a large piece of bone.

Now he walked with a slight limp. To make matters worse, the wound gave him problems during major changes in the weather. By the feel of his leg, Windham knew that tonight's storm would be the worst of the summer.

So far the drive up from southern Texas toward Abilene had gone without serious trouble. Two stampedes and one drover drowned in the Brazos; forty head given to the Kiowa to cross the Nations. Things could have been a lot worse. No one had been shot yet.

This had surprised Windham, whose job was to protect the herd from thieves. He carried a Colt Army .44 in a fringed leather holster at his side, and rode a Spencer repeating rifle in a finely tooled scabbard. He had spent more time cleaning the weapons than actually using them.

He had emptied his Colt turning the herd during the last stampede, and a rattler in his bedroll north of Fort Worth had taken but one shot. Seven bullets in five hundred miles wasn't worth talking about.

Windham had known the rattler had been put in his bed as a joke. He had thought about aiming his Colt at the drover's toes. But it had all been in good fun, and no harm was done.

Windham had learned to live with practical jokes, even if they came from ex-Confederates. Most of the drovers from Texas had fought in a gray uniform.

In trying to put the war behind him, Windham had drifted to his cousin's J7 outfit near San Antonio. Skip Halvorson, who had worn a Confederate uniform, was gaining a reputation as a top rancher and would be one of the first to send beef to the new stockyards in Abilene, Kansas.

Halvorson knew the drive would be risky and had been glad to see Windham, the cousin he had faced across the trenches at Shiloh. They had stood, braced to shoot one another. Both had put their rifles on someone else.

With the war past, Halvorson had wanted Windham on his side from now on. Windham could help him. They could help each other.

Windham gulped another mouthful of coffee as the

last light faded and the rumbling grew louder. Beside him sat Jake Malone, a rawboned Texan nearing thirty, who had also been hired more for his ability with a gun than a rope.

"We've had it good so far," Malone commented. "My gut says things are going to get real hard from here on. And I don't mean just that storm that's boiling in, either."

Windham knew exactly what Malone meant. While scouting earlier in the day, they had cut the tracks of nearly a dozen riders. Fresh campfire ashes had led them both to believe that a gang was riding parallel to the herd, waiting for a chance to strike.

"They aren't Indians," Malone had said. "I'd say they're thieves, waiting for a chance at our herd."

Slack Cardwell, the trail boss, rode into camp. He stepped his big frame down from the saddle and took a cup of coffee from the cook, frowning at the sky.

"We're in for a bad one, boys. I should write a letter home."

"Tonight won't be no picnic," Malone agreed. "Like they say, if there's trouble, you'll find it on the Cimarron."

"If we can just keep them from running south," Cardwell said, "we can likely hold them together. If they get started on us, they'll go clean to hell before we catch them."

"*To* hell?" Malone said. "I thought we were already there."

Cardwell and Malone had both been up the trail the year before, in '68, with one of the first herds to the new Kansas railheads. They had braved the scare of Spanish fever among the herds and had sold a lot of longhorns to an enterprising man named Joseph McCoy, who had built a stockyard at Abilene.

People in the East wanted beef and there were thousands of wild longhorns to be roped and herded north. Those with ambition, and a bit of recklessness, could make themselves some money—if they could avoid serious trouble.

The worst enemy was the weather. Thunderstorms generally meant stampedes. A bad run could ruin an entire trail drive. It could take weeks to round up all the steers.

Now the threat of thieves on top of it meant more trouble than a trail crew could handle.

Cardwell and Malone continued to complain about the oncoming storm. Windham stared into the sky. "I'll get out with the herd," he told Cardwell. "I expect you'll need us all tonight."

Malone volunteered to help with the remuda, the horse herd. He stood up and started out of camp, frowning at the flashing light overhead.

Usually Windham and Malone slept nights and scouted throughout the days. Ordinarily, they rode out early to check the country ahead and look for possible trouble. Tonight there was trouble everywhere.

Cardwell watched Malone disappear toward the remuda. He moved next to Windham, sipping noisily on his coffee, more worried about thieves than the weather.

"Jake says you and he cut tracks out from camp," Cardwell said. "What do you think?"

"It's not good," Windham answered. "They're not driving cattle or horses. We figure they're looking to take some of ours."

"Are there too many for us to handle?"

"Depends on how determined they are," Windham said. "They don't hide themselves well and that means they're either not trail wise or they don't care who knows they're around. I'd say it was the latter."

"We'll likely know soon enough," Cardwell said, looking into the storm. "Everything's about to bust open on us."

Windham finished his coffee and grabbed his saddle. All the regular cowhands were already at the remuda, choosing their horses. Though everyone was bone tired, there would be no sleep for anyone tonight.

Lightning flashed heavier and a gusty wind filled with rain spattered Windham's face. He watched while the wrangler culled his red pinto, Checkers, from the remuda.

Charlie Graham was as good with horses as a man could get. Barely eighteen, he had been comfortable riding before he could walk. He had kept the horses together and well broken throughout the drive.

"You're slick with a rope, Charlie," Windham said. "You don't care, dark of night, or wind, or whatever, you drop that loop real fine."

Graham led Windham's pinto over, smiling, holding his hat on with his free hand. "I've got no say in the weather. It's a damned nuisance right now."

"It's more than a nuisance," another cowhand remarked. "From what I can see, the good Lord is plumb upset tonight."

Stick Mason had been with the drive since its beginning. Tall, lean, and Negro, he was considered one of the top hands, willing to work more than his share to show his gratitude for the job. "The boss man give me a chance when others wouldn't," he would always say. "Least I can do is care properly for his stock."

Though Stick credited Cardwell with giving him a job, it was the wrangler, Charlie Graham, who had exerted his influence. "Stick raised me from the time I was six, after my folks passed on," he had told Cardwell in confidence. "He was like a father to me, and taught me most of what I know about horses. I don't want to wrangle for you if Stick can't go along."

Stick had been hired and those who couldn't live with it had left. There were a lot of hard feelings from the war, but no man asked another about his past unless he wanted trouble.

The hands were a mixture of Mexican vaqueros and young Texans who'd fought in Rebel uniforms. Along the trail, there were others who didn't like Stick being in the outfit. One by one, they had left.

The rest respected Stick Mason for his candid views on life, and never called him names behind his back.

Windham threw the saddle over his pinto. Stick Mason motioned toward a roan gelding, one of a set of two that he owned. He watched Charlie Graham rope the roan and lead it from the herd.

"Try and stay on, Stick," Graham said with a laugh. "It's going to be a bumpy night."

Stick saddled the mare and pointed into the sky. "I feel the Lord's wrath coming down on us. It's going to be the worst night we've seen. The worst by far."

A flash of lightning broke the darkness. "Hold your tongue, Stick," Graham said. "You'll bring us all bad luck."

"I've got nothing to do with our luck," Stick said. "It's already come to us. Nothing I can say's going to change it."

"But I'd rather you not dwell on it," Charlie said. "I've got the shakes as it is."

Stick turned to Windham. "What do you think, Mr. Gunman? I noticed you limping pretty bad."

"Things don't feel good to me," Windham said. "But

an old fur trader once told me, 'If trouble's for certain, try to enjoy it.' "

Stick laughed. "I figure we'll have plenty to enjoy."

"You two are a lot of comfort," Charlie Graham said.

Windham mounted his pinto. "There won't be any comfort for anyone until sunup, Charlie. And maybe not even then."

TWO

WINDHAM RODE with Stick Mason toward the herd. The cattle were milling and bawling, their wild eyes rolling. Thunder boomed louder and closer. The rain increased and jagged light streaked to the ground, white hot, filling the air with a pungent smell.

Stick and Windham joined other cowhands gathering at the south end of the herd. The storm had come down-river, from the northwest, and the steers were getting set to push their way through the line of drovers.

Slack Cardwell rode along the line, yelling, "Push them east! Push them east! We'll turn them up north when we've got them moving."

Cardwell was too late. A flash of white streaked into the herd, dropping a steer. Suddenly a ball of static light began rolling from one set of horns to another. The herd bolted.

Cowboys yelled and spurred their horses away from the line. Windham's pony, knowing the sound of a stampede from buffalo hunts, spun on its back hooves as a wave of terrified steers bore down through the darkness.

Windham held fast as the pinto broke into a dead run. The steers were coming hard, but the pony's speed carried Windham far out in front of the herd.

The storm boomed overhead and each crack of thunder made the steers run even faster. There was no telling how far the herd would go or when they would stop.

Like the other hands, Windham turned his winded horse out and around from the front of the stampede, into a grove of live oak, while the herd roared past.

Cardwell and a number of other hands joined Windham. Cardwell was cursing.

"Boss, you had just as well save your breath," Stick Mason remarked. "The good Lord has his ways."

"Well, I'm not happy about it," Cardwell said.

Another cowhand, riding from the direction of camp, raced his horse to a stop near Cardwell. "You've all got to come up and help!" he yelled. "Thieves have gotten the horses!"

"What?" Cardwell cursed again. "What about Jake Malone and Charlie Graham?"

"They're trying to catch the thieves," the hand replied. "They're going to get themselves killed."

Cardwell picked Windham and Stick Mason to ride back with him, and ordered the others to follow the herd.

"I'm no gunhand," Stick protested. "But if you think it's the Lord's wish . . ."

"It's the Lord's wish," Cardwell said. "And it's mine, too, since I give the orders."

Windham rode with his pistol drawn. It would be an

open fight with the thieves, the kind of horseback dueling he had learned very well with the Cheyenne.

Windham had developed the Indian instinct for survival. He wore buckskins and rode Indian ponies, not the newer crossbreeds that were coming from the racing stock. He wanted a horse that could turn on a dime and live through the winter on range grass.

To Windham, fighting on horseback beat retreating on the ground any day. And having the right kind of pony made all the difference in the world.

Windham held his pistol up. Stick rode beside him, pulling a Colt Dragoon from his waistband. "I'm praying for a steady hand. I'm praying hard. But I don't need to pray for you; I know your hand is steady."

"Pray for me anyway," Windham said. "I could use it."

Rain was falling heavily, making vision difficult. With the flashes of lightning, they could see the horse herd being driven away in the distance.

They reined in where the remuda had been held and everyone began yelling and pointing. Doubled over on the ground was one of the hands.

Cardwell jumped down from his horse and shouted up at Stick and Windham, "They got Charlie! Damn them, they've shot Charlie Graham!"

A short distance away, flashes of gunfire were visible through the rain. Jake Malone was trying to stop the thieves alone. Windham and Stick turned their horses and rode full speed through the storm.

Windham counted five thieves who had doubled back from the main group. The thieves formed a skirmish line and began pouring gunfire toward Stick and Windham.

Jake Malone was doubled over in the saddle, holding

his left shoulder. His horse bolted and he fell to the ground.

Leaning over his pinto, Windham charged the outlaws from the side. Screaming loudly, he rode directly toward a thief. Startled, the thief tried to turn his horse, but too late. Windham was upon him.

As Windham rode by, he leveled his Colt and fired point-blank into the outlaw's chest. The thief yelled and flipped backward out of the saddle.

Stick Mason's Dragoon belched flame three, four, then five times. An outlaw fell shooting at him. Another fired wildly, hitting Stick's roan in the neck. The horse staggered, screaming, and fell. Stick rolled free and limped toward cover.

The three remaining thieves turned their fire toward Windham, who was crouched over his pinto, riding in a zigzag line toward them through the darkness.

Windham picked one and bore down. Too late, the thief turned his horse to escape. Windham rode alongside and shot broadside into his head, blowing him out of the saddle.

The remaining two turned their horses and rode away as hard as they could. Windham followed, emptying his Colt at them.

After a short chase, Windham reined his pony to a stop. It was useless to continue. Even with a number of men, he could never catch up to the main body of thieves in the darkness. The remuda was gone.

The storm began to lessen, passing south. A nearly full moon broke free of the clouds, bathing the Cimarron in a soft light. Soon the crickets were chirping and the country turned as peaceful as it had been turbulent.

Windham found Malone sitting on a log, holding his shoulder. Stick was trying to help Malone to his feet, but was struggling himself, unable to put full weight on his right leg.

"You sure shot the hell out of them," Stick told Windham. "I think my praying helped."

"I believe it, Stick. But what about you and Jake?"

"It's my ankle," Stick said. "It's not broke, but I sure twisted it going down with my horse."

Windham turned to Malone. "How bad is your shoulder?"

"Just grazed the bone," Malone said. "I pulled some splinters out, but nothing's broke. I was lucky."

"I aim to trail those thieves come first light," Windham told them. "We can't afford to lose those horses."

"I'll wrap this shoulder and go with you," Malone said.

"I doubt you can travel. Not hard, anyway. Besides, Cardwell will need someone here to gunhawk the herd. We can't both be gone at the same time."

Malone got to his feet. "It was my fault they took the horses. I should've opened fire when I first saw them."

"No," Windham said. "You don't go shooting in the dark."

"You can't blame yourself," Stick added. "Mr. Windham's right. No sane man goes shooting until he knows what he's shooting at."

"I had a gut feeling it was trouble," Malone said. "If I'd shot them up and asked questions later, they wouldn't have gotten Charlie."

Stick continued to argue. "You don't know any such thing for certain, Jake. The Lord has his ways."

"Would you stop with the Lord stuff?" Malone said.

Stick nodded. "If it makes you feel better. But just the same, He'll tend to things as He sees fit."

Windham caught Jake Malone's horse and helped him back into the saddle. "You sure you can ride?" he asked.

"I've been shot worse than this," Malone said. "You help Stick. I'll see you back in camp."

Stick was over talking to his fallen horse. Windham waited until he was finished. Stick limped over, wiping his eyes. "I never figured to lose him like this. His brother's gone now, too. Those thieves got the two best horses I ever owned."

"Get on my pinto," Windham offered. "We'll get back to camp and figure things out."

"Nothing against your pinto, Mr. Windham," Stick said, "but I'll walk, thank you."

"You shouldn't be on that ankle," Windham insisted.

"I'm not riding no other horse till Jefferson is buried proper," Stick said. "They've got Jackson out there somewhere. I can't do nothing about that. But I want to bury Jefferson proper."

Windham knew how much Stick's twin roan geldings meant to him. Losing one of them like this would be hard on him for some time to come.

Windham helped Stick cut a crutch from an oak sapling. Stick said nothing about his injured ankle, but Windham could tell he was in considerable pain. So far, the night had been worse than he had predicted. Windham wondered what else lay in store before the sun broke again.

Three

IN CAMP, everyone was gathered near the chuck wagon. Some of the younger drovers had their hands over their faces, crying.

Jake Malone, his right shoulder bound tightly, greeted Stick and Windham. "They're saying that Charlie's wound is mortal. He's gut-shot. He likely won't last the night."

Stick turned and limped away. He stood staring up into the sky. Then he made his way over to his bedroll and belongings, and began to rummage around.

Windham followed Malone to where Charlie Graham lay near the chuck wagon, covered by saddle blankets. Moss Mitchell, the cook, was wiping sweat from Graham's brow.

Windham knelt down at Graham's side. The wrangler was short of breath as he spoke.

"Mr. Windham, I didn't figure it to end this way."

"Don't give it up, Charlie," Windham said. "It's not over yet."

"Not by a damn site," Stick said, pushing his way past cowhands to Graham's side.

"Stick," Graham said. "It's good to see you. They said you lost Jefferson."

"You don't worry about a thing now, you hear?" Stick said. "I'm going to fix you up. You just rest quiet."

Stick pulled back Graham's covers and checked his wound. The bullet had entered to the right and just above the navel, and had passed straight through, narrowly missing the spine.

Stick opened a skin bag and took out a handful of dried plants. He handed them to the cook. "You heat these up in a little water. I'm going out and get some more plants and roots that we'll need. Then we'll pack everything on both sides of the wound."

Stick hobbled over to Charlie Graham's horse and mounted. Soon he was lost in the darkness.

"That Stick is one-of-a-kind," a short cowhand named Gilman remarked. "His ankle's hurt bad, yet he don't let on. He figures he can save Charlie. And I'll bet he can."

"What Charlie needs is some real doctoring," said another hand, a wiry cowboy named Carter. "Not some witch-doctoring and such."

"Are *you* a real doctor?" Gilman asked.

"No, I ain't. But we ought to go get one."

Gilman was trembling with rage. "Do you see one sitting around here close? Maybe there's one over the hill, just waiting for us."

"We need to *find* one," Carter said.

"Should we just sit back and do nothing while we

hunt one down?" Gilman persisted. "Should we just let Charlie die without doing anything?"

Carter was glaring down on Gilman. "I figure he'll die for certain if Stick sets to witch-doctoring him."

"What do you know about it?" Gilman asked. "You ain't smart enough to know your own turds from plug tobacco."

The two hands began fighting. Cardwell broke them up, saying, "A fine way of handling our problems here. Charlie's shot and the horses are gone. The herd's south of here, run to hell and back with the storm, and all you two can do is fight."

"He's got no right to say that about Stick," Gilman insisted. "We all know Stick will do right by Charlie."

"I'm saying none of us can help by fighting," Cardwell said. "It's time to get back to work. Charlie needs rest and there's a lot of beeves out there in the dark someplace."

"Charlie's my friend," Gilman said. "I want to stay with him."

"You can't help him," Cardwell said. "Get on your horse." He waved his arm in a circle. "All of you, get out there and find those steers. I don't want anyone back until the herd's together. You all understand?"

Gilman and Carter picked up their hats and the others followed them out of camp. Soon they were all mounted and riding south under a moonlit sky.

"You needn't have been so hard on them," Graham told Cardwell. He coughed. "Things have all gone crazy around here. No one knows what to do."

"You do as Stick says and just rest," Cardwell said. "You're in no condition to be worrying about anything. I'll do the bossing around here. Things'll work out."

Windham stood off with Jake Malone, watching. Cardwell came over, his hands on his hips.

"We need to go out and help them round up the herd," he said. "I figure we'd better have those steers back together by noon tomorrow, or this drive's a bust."

"I'm going after the horses," Windham said.

"Oh, really?"

"I have to."

"What do you figure you can do alone?" Cardwell asked.

"I believe if I pick them off one by one, maybe they'll turn tail and run. Then I'll drive the horses back."

"And if they come after you?" Cardwell said. "You're a good fighter, Frank, but there are way too many of them."

"I've got to try," Windham said. "It's my job. I can't let Skip down."

"Skip's not about to hold you accountable. He's got more horses than he knows what to do with."

"I need to go, just the same. It's my job."

"Your job is to do what I tell you," Cardwell said. "I've got some cash stored in case of emergency. We'll pick up enough horses along the way to make it to Abilene. It's not a problem."

"It could be a problem if these thieves steal horses along the way. There won't be any left for us."

"We'll find some somewhere, Frank. Rest easy."

"I can't," Windham said. "We lost a lot of good horseflesh. It's not fair to the hands."

Cardwell blew out his breath. "Frank, you can't take this on yourself. You've done your job. Both you and Jake have done way better than most. That's why we haven't had this problem yet. Blame it on the storm; that's what caused this."

"Maybe, but I should have been watching out better," Windham said. "I should have known this would happen."

"You went with the rest of us to hold the herd, where you thought you were needed most," Cardwell said. "And that's where you *were* needed most. You're not to blame."

Stick Mason yelled from just outside of camp. He rode in and tossed a bag of roots at Moss Mitchell's feet.

"Set to steaming them real slow," he told Mitchell. "I'll be back to help just as soon as I show the boss what I found."

Cardwell turned to Stick. "What is it?"

Stick pointed north of camp. "I found another thief, wounded, crawling through the trees. He's not about to go nowhere, though. I tied him up good."

The hands started talking among themselves. One of them help up a rope.

"We don't need everyone out there," Cardwell said. "Stick said there was one man."

"He says he's a Jayhawker," Stick said to Cardwell. "You might want to hear what he's got to say about our horses."

Cardwell calmed the hands down once again. "Everyone stay here and get ready to go after beeves. I'm taking Windham and Stick with me, no one else. I want that understood."

"You aim to hang him?" one of the hands asked.

"We'll take care of him," Cardwell said. "I want everyone ready to ride hard when I get back. Losing the horses is the least of our worries."

Four

WINDHAM LEFT with Stick and Cardwell. Out from camp, at the edge of the trees, they found a young outlaw in his late teens. Stick had tied him to a young oak. He was bleeding badly, his right thigh shattered by a bullet.

"He's lost a lot of blood," Stick commented. "Too much."

"I must have hit him when I was firing wild," Windham said. "I would never have guessed any of them were this young."

"He's too young to be a Jayhawker," Cardwell noted.

"I ain't too young," the outlaw said, shouting in a raspy voice. "There's others younger than me."

"The war's been over four years," Stick pointed out.

"Not for us," the outlaw spat. "We aim to keep them Confederate cattle from coming up into our country, ruining things. No grayback Texans are going to make money off'n our land."

"You won't be stopping any herds from now on," Cardwell said.

"You aim to hang me, don't you?" the outlaw said.

"Any reason why we shouldn't?" Cardwell asked.

"I can tell you about your horses. Where they're going."

"Start talking," Cardwell said.

"I want your word you won't hang me."

"I'm not giving you my word on nothing."

The kid crossed his arms. "Then I don't aim to tell you anything."

"They left you to die," Windham pointed out. "Why should you stand by them?"

The kid pointed at Windham. "It weren't their fault. It was yours. You shot us all up."

Windham turned to Cardwell. "Let's just hang him."

Cardwell started for his horse.

"Wait!" the kid said. "Listen, I'll tell you if you don't hang me. I will."

Cardwell stood over the kid, knowing he was close to death anyway. "I won't hang you, kid. I promise. Tell us what you know."

The kid's voice began to falter. "Will you get me to a doc?"

"I said I wouldn't hang you."

"Then I ain't telling you nothing." His breath was shallow, barely above a whisper.

"We're wasting our time here," Windham said. "You said you wouldn't hang him, so we won't. We'll do what he asks and leave him. The wolves will find him. He'd better pray they find him before the Kiowa or Comanche."

"Wait." The kid struggled to one elbow. "Look, I

know I'm near dead. I can feel it. I just didn't think they'd leave me like that." He began to sob. "They just rode off and left me."

"You don't owe them a thing," Windham repeated. "Why did you join up with them?"

The kid wiped his eyes. "I never figured it was right. I just hated that my pa got killed in the war. Everyone I knew was gone—dead or moved away. Ma left with some man and didn't take me. I had no one. These men said I could ride with them."

The kid was sobbing again. He tried to talk, but his sorrow drained him of his strength. Suddenly his mouth opened in a last gasp for air, and he died.

Cardwell took a deep breath. "God forgive me, I wanted to shoot him. I was so mad I wanted to just blow his head off."

"He was a kid," Windham said, "but he was one of them. It might have been his bullet that got Charlie."

"He was shooting with the rest of them," Stick said. "He would have killed any one of us, no question."

"I wish he'd have talked about the horses," Cardwell said. "Now we don't know any more than when we came out here."

"He told me a few things before I came back to camp," Stick said. "He talked about a hideout along the Arkansas River, somewhere east of Fort Dodge. Maybe that's where they took the horses."

"It's possible," Windham said. "It's a start. I'll know where to head for, at least."

"I thought I told you that you weren't going," Cardwell said.

"You know me, Slack," Windham said. "I've got the scent now. I want those horses back."

"I'm going with you," Stick said. "You can't go alone, and I need my other horse back."

Cardwell turned to Stick and pointed at him. "*You* for sure are *not* going. You'll stay here and help with the herd."

"Jefferson's gone," Stick said. "I've got to get Jackson back."

"You'll use Charlie's horse," Cardwell said. "We need your help. We're shorthanded as it is."

"I need to go," Stick insisted. "I need to help Frank."

"I said you're staying!" Cardwell yelled. "I've tried to talk Frank out of it. If he wants to get himself killed, then I won't stop him. But you're coming with me and help gather that herd. Or whatever is left of it. Some how, some way, I'm getting that stock north. It's going to happen."

Back in camp, Stick helped Moss Mitchell tie the herb poultices over Charlie's wounds. He instructed Moss on how to feed Charlie the roots, all the while watching Windham pack his saddlebags with dried beef and hard biscuits.

Windham was throwing his saddlebags over his horse when Stick came up behind him. "Don't you leave here without me. You hear? I'll never forgive you."

Windham turned. "Cardwell told you to stay with the herd."

"To hell with that! It's the Lord's will I go with you."

"What if he tries to stop you?"

"He'll have the Lord to contend with."

"I'll have Cardwell to answer to if you come," Windham said. "He yells a whole lot louder."

"Listen, I'm staying behind to bury Jefferson," Stick said. "When I'm done, I'll catch up with you. No two ways about it."

Windham tightened down his saddlebag in silence. Stick grabbed the strap on the saddlebag and held it fast, glaring at Windham.

"Tell me you'll wait for me, Frank. Tell me!"

"Cardwell's the boss, Stick. I can't speak for him."

"I'm not asking you to. I'm asking you to wait for me. Will you do that?"

"Okay, I'll wait for you, Stick," Windham said. "I'll be up at the main crossing on the Cimarron. I'll wait until sunup. No longer."

Stick released the saddlebag. "I thank you, Frank. You'll be glad."

"And we never had this conversation," Windham said. "You just caught up with me. Understand?"

Stick raised his right hand. "Only the Lord and I thought it up. You had nothing to do with it." He struggled atop Charlie Graham's horse. "I'll see you there before daylight. Then we'll go get us some Jayhawkers."

Five

AWN WAS a streak of crimson along the Cimarron. Windham crouched in the shadows, his pistol drawn. He had heard a horse and rider coming toward the river. He would soon know if it was Stick Mason.

Stick approached the crossing carefully, watching in all directions. Just out from the crossing, he sat the horse and waited for Windham.

One thing Stick had learned about Frank Windham: he was quiet and he was never in a hurry to reveal himself.

Windham finally rode from the trees. "I wasn't sure you'd make it, Stick."

"I wasn't sure, either," Stick said. "I just about didn't get away."

"Slack caught you leaving, is that it?"

"Slack helped me bury Jefferson," Stick explained.

"He's an awfully nice man, but he and I don't think alike. Not a-tall."

"He let you come, though. He didn't stop you."

"No. You see, I had to quit."

"You had to quit?"

"He wasn't about to let me come, no matter what. So I told him I quit. That way he couldn't hold me."

"So he just let you come, without saying anything?"

"Oh, he said plenty," Stick said. "Most of it wasn't too nice, neither. I told him the Lord was listening. He didn't care, not even a little bit."

"What are you going to do without a job?" Windham asked.

"I figure he'll hire me again when we get the horses back," Stick said. "I'm not worried. He shouldn't be, either."

"He's worried about you getting shot, Stick. That's what it's all about."

"I've been shot before," Stick said. "Won't be nothing new."

They crossed the Cimarron, following the trail left by the Jayhawkers. The trail was wide and deeply marked, due to the thunderstorm. Stick and Windham rode carefully, in case one or more of the thieves had doubled back.

Windham had gotten along well with Stick during the entire drive. Once, when a young vaquero had been snakebitten, Windham had helped Stick gather roots to mix as a poultice, to pull the poison out. Stick was always there to help.

Windham had often thought about Stick and the others like him who had been freed by the war. Their lives had changed in some ways; but there had really been no freedom.

Yet Stick had never been one to complain. He could hold his own with any man, be the test physical or mental. Windham wondered if this trip wasn't going to be his hardest test.

At midday, they approached a series of hollows set within groves of oak and hickory. Just beyond the next ridge, a thin film of smoke curled into the sky.

Windham took the lead. They rode to where they could see the remains of a small cabin. A lone man was sitting with his back against a tree, staring into the ruins.

Stick and Windham approached cautiously. The man's hair was thick, just beginning to gray, and matted with dried blood. His left side was wide open, and he was holding his intestines in as best he could.

"My God!" Stick said. "What happened here?"

"Go ahead and finish me," the dying man said. "I'm not long for this world, anyway. Jayhawkers seen to that. They came late last night; took my wife and daughter. My daughter's of age and they'll ruin her. Just shoot me. Do it."

"If you'll lay back, maybe I can sew you shut," Stick offered.

The man put a bloody hand out to push Stick away. "I don't want the likes of you to touch me. How do I know you're not one of them?"

"Do you figure I'd cut you and then sew you up, all in the same day?" Stick asked.

"Maybe so." He looked to Windham. "You would seem to be part Injun, by your dress. You aim to cut me up worse?"

"You can't be cut up worse," Windham said. "I've lived with Indians. I know; you couldn't be cut up worse." Windham knelt down beside him. "Let my friend help you. What have you got to lose?"

"Just let me die in peace."

"We came after horses we lost to Jayhawkers," Windham said. "They were likely the same bunch. We're after them, not you."

The man stared hard at Windham. "I still don't believe you."

"Think about it," Windham said. "Why would we come back? What's here for us?"

"I figure maybe you know about Jenny and Jessie."

"Jenny and Jessie?"

"I don't want you to take them," the dying man said. "You'd best go. She can shoot, Jenny can. If she'd been here before, you couldn't have done this. You couldn't."

"Believe me," Windham said, "we're not here to harm you. Why don't you let us help?"

The man stared straight ahead. "Git on out of here, both of you. And leave Jenny and Jessie alone."

"Look, we don't know nothing about no Jenny and Jessie," Stick put in, "but you're about to die for sure if you don't let me tend to you."

"Let him help you," Windham said. "He knows doctoring. Give yourself a chance."

"They ripped me open with my own knife," the man said. "I know better than to think I've got a chance. But I don't aim to let you harm any more of my kin."

Windham stood up. "Let's ride on. We haven't got time for this."

"He'll die for sure," Stick said.

"That's what he wants, it appears," Windham said. "Mount up. We've got a lot of ground to cover."

Windham climbed into the saddle. Stick slipped on his bad ankle, just as rifle fire opened up from the trees. He dropped to one knee as his horse jerked wildly, a bullet hole in its neck.

The horse went down, squealing loudly. Stick rolled clear and pulled his Colt Dragoon.

Windham slid from his pinto. He took cover behind

the tree where the dying man sat slurring, "I told you she could shoot. I told you. You'll both get it now."

"Her days are about over," Windham said. "The Indians taught me about brush fighting. You'd best call off the shooting."

"I'll see you die first," the man said.

Stick was lying flat on the ground, cringing as bullets ripped the sod next to him. He raised his Dragoon and fired into the trees in front of him.

Windham fired two shots and ran into a thick grove of young oak. Stick fired twice more. When Windham saw movement in the brush, he took careful aim.

His shot brought a cry and a string of curses. The dying man, holding his distended stomach, began yelling for no more shooting.

"Jenny! Jessie!" he yelled. "Don't shoot no more!"

There was the sound of a boy's whimpering from the trees, and a woman's voice trying to quiet and comfort him. Windham worked his way closer to them.

"Come out, Jennie!" the man yelled. "One of them's in the tress after you. He knows Injun ways. He'll kill you both."

Two figures appeared from the trees. A young woman in a weathered riding skirt and a shirt, and a worn hat over long blonde hair, held a Henry .44 repeating rifle above her head. She helped a boy who was holding his arm.

Windham came out of the trees, his Spencer leveled. He told the woman to drop her rifle and move away from it.

"Don't shoot," the woman said. "We thought you were Jayhawkers."

"We're not," Windham said. He pointed to the dying man. "He won't let us help him."

The woman and the wounded boy hurried to the dying man's side. "Uncle Rex," she said, "they've killed you, too."

The man was slumped over, his eyes clouded and filmy. Windham helped the woman lay him flat, then closed his eyes.

"No man deserves to die that way," Windham said.

"They'll pay for it," the woman said matter-of-factly. "They'll pay dearly."

"How bad is the boy?" Windham asked.

"He's no boy." She brushed tears from her cheeks. "It's an arm wound. He'll live."

Windham motioned over to where Stick was tending to the boy. "He'll care for him. You needn't worry. You must be Jenny."

"I'm Jenny," she said, turning to the smoldering ruins. "Everything's gone to hell."

"My name's Frank Windham, and that's my partner, Stick Mason. We've come from a trail herd, chasing Jayhawkers that stole our horses. I'm sorry we had to come upon this."

Windham studied the woman's face. She was likely in her mid twenties, wise to the ways of open country. Dirt and anger hid her beauty.

"We thought you were with them," she said. "I'm sorry about that." She walked over and picked up her rifle. "I don't see any more bodies out here. Karlie and Aunt June must be in the ashes. I guess we'd just as well bury them with Uncle Rex."

"Your uncle said the Jayhawkers took them," Windham told her.

Jenny's face paled. "You certain?"

"He was certain. I just listened."

"They're better off dead." She walked into the trees and led out a pack horse. She untied a shovel and walked toward Windham. "I'm doing this too often lately. The next time I use a shovel, I'll be burying one of those men."

Six

WINDHAM HELPED Jenny Parson bury her uncle. She insisted on doing most of the digging, using a small trench shovel her uncle had brought back from the war. She buried him deep, mounding it heavily over the top.

Standing over the grave, she bit her lip until it bled. She turned to Windham and wiped her eyes.

"Jessie and I are going with you."

Windham frowned. "That's not a good idea."

"I don't care about your ideas. We're going."

"The trail is no place for you or the boy."

"He's not a boy. He's twelve and he's got spunk."

"Twelve's too young to die."

"We've got nothing else," Jenny argued. "We had a place back across the gulch, but the Jayhawkers burned us out. They killed my husband. Jessie and I would have died as well, except we were in town."

"I'm sorry," Windham said. "I didn't know."

"There's a lot you don't know, Mr. Windham, not if you think you're going to keep us from coming with you."

"What do you expect to gain?" Windham asked.

"Karlie and Aunt June are all the kin we've got," Jenny said. "I would like to at least try and find them. They deserve that much."

"You might not like what you find."

"I'll take my chances, Mr. Windham. It couldn't be worse than what I've already found."

"You have a point," Windham acknowledged. "I'll need to warn you, though, we'll be riding fast. Few stops and little to eat."

"That sounds good to me."

"And there'll be shooting."

"The more the better. If your friend Stick hadn't slipped on his bad ankle mounting his horse, we'd have buried him, too, and the horse would be alive."

Windham's eyes narrowed. "You'd have filled a grave as well, miss. Stick's as close to me as blood kin. You'll remember that."

"I've got nothing against him," Jenny said. "But I saw him standing over my gut-stuck uncle. You've got to realize how I felt."

"How do you feel about Stick in general?" Windham asked. "Have you got anything against his kind?"

"Mr. Windham," Jenny replied, "I was married to one of 'his kind.' "

Windham stared. "I meant no offense."

"Of course you didn't. You've never heard of such a thing, have you?"

"Not in these parts."

"In what parts is it common, Mr. Windham?"

"None that I know of," Windham said. "Let's get your brother taken care of and ride out of here."

Stick was busy pressing a poultice and wrap around Jessie's arm. Jessie eyed Windham suspiciously.

"Sorry I shot you, son," Windham said. "But I don't figure on dying anytime soon. It appeared that you and your sister had it in for Stick and me."

Jessie nodded. He stared over at his uncle's grave. Jenny put an arm around him. "We're going with them. We've got to find Karlie and Aunt June. You buck up, now, y'hear?"

Jessie continued to stare at the grave.

"Y'hear, Jessie?" Jenny shook him. "We've got work to do. You and me and these two men. We'll work together."

"If you say so," Jessie said. "We'd best get on, then."

As Jenny had shot Stick's horse, he rode hers. She would have it no other way. Jenny rode double with Jessie on his horse, a strong little dun named Molly.

Jenny tied the small shovel to the horse, saying that she had vowed to bury Jayhawkers. "I figure this will help me keep my word," she said.

Windham was frustrated. He knew they wouldn't be able to even keep up with the thieves, let alone gain on them. Their only chance would be to buy a horse from someone willing to sell.

That would be difficult, as everyone in these parts needed horses, and few had any to spare.

Windham knew it was their only chance, though. Jenny and Jessie couldn't ride double forever and expect the mare to hold up. They would need to find another horse soon—if there were any that hadn't been stolen by Jayhawkers.

Noon came with Windham sitting his pinto on a high hill, looking for signs of the thieves. Below, Stick worked to check the bleeding from Jessie's arm. They had stopped a number of times for the same thing.

Throughout the ordeal, Jessie had never complained, though he had cast averted glances at Windham, wondering if he still wanted to kill him.

Jenny had told Jessie a number of times to forget about it, that Windham had acted to save Stick and himself. "It was nothing personal against you. He just didn't want to get shot by us."

Windham came down from the hill. Jessie stared at him all the way, patting his horse, Molly, on the neck.

"Would you stop it, Jessie," Jenny said. "That's downright rude."

Everyone dismounted and Windham led the way to a small spring, where they watered their horses. Jessie continued to stare at Windham.

Jenny elbowed her brother. "Jessie, what did I tell you?"

"I'm not afraid of Mr. Windham shooting me again," Jessie said. "I just wonder how he could have shot me in the first place. He limps nearly worse than Mr. Stick."

"Never be fooled by what you think you see," Windham advised. "I knew a man with a wooden leg who could outrun a horse."

Stick leaned over toward Windham. "The Lord don't like them who lie," he whispered.

"Did you say a one-legged man outran a horse?" Jessie asked.

"That's right," Windham said. "Beat him by a full length."

"I don't believe that," Jessie said.

"Suit yourself," Windham told him. "But I wouldn't bet on it if I were you."

"How about if *I* bet you?" Stick asked.

Jessie led his horse to drink and turned to Windham.

"You're funnin' me, ain't you. I mean, about the man with one leg."

"I'm just saying you can't be certain of anything," Windham said. "Don't make up your mind about things being just so. You don't have room for change."

The dun pulled up from drinking and snorted. Jessie rubbed its neck. "Mr. Windham, did you want to kill me back at my uncle's cabin?"

"No," Windham replied. "Your sister is right: I just wanted to save myself."

"How did you get lost in the trees so easily? I didn't even know where you were, and I know the woods real well."

"I lived with the Cheyenne for a time," Windham explained, "when I was about your age. It was a hard life, but I feel now that I owe them a lot. I'd be dead now if I hadn't learned how to fight from them."

"Jenny shoots as good as anybody," Jessie said. "Still, she couldn't find you to get off a shot. She couldn't even *see* you in them trees. How did you do that?"

Windham explained that the Cheyenne had taught him how to become a part of his surroundings, to blend in and not be seen.

"It's something you have to learn," Windham said. "It's hard and it takes a lot of practice."

"Could you teach *me* how to do that?" Jessie asked.

"If you're willing. If you're patient."

"I'm used to hard work, Mr. Windham. I just want to live and help my sister stay alive, too."

Stick, who had been listening, told Jessie, "If it's the Lord's will, you'll live, no matter what."

"I figure on living," Jessie said. "I've got a score to settle with some Jayhawkers. Injun training will give me an edge. Likely a big edge."

Seven

WINDHAM LED the way through hilly country filled with brush and studded with cedars. The hills occasionally broke into large parks, where the grass grew stirrup high.

The Jayhawkers' trail was easy to follow: a long, twisting line of trampled grass that stayed to the roughest part of the area. Windham could see, now and again, where the horses had spread out to graze, but only where the thieves could post sentries on nearby hills.

Windham believed the gang's main core was made up of hardened ex-soldiers, men who had seen a lot of fighting during the war and knew how to survive. Likely they had been Jayhawkers during the war, an irregular band of outlaws that fought without just cause, pillaging and killing for the pure fun of it.

After the South's defeat, these killers had continued their predation in the region. Now the trail herds were

another target. The older members were teaching the
newcomers the skills needed to continue thieving and
killing.

Windham knew their ways. He had fought against a
similar group of thieves in northern Kansas, just after
the close of the war. They had tried to hold up a supply
train he had been guarding. He had killed their leader,
a man named Kelly Barrett, and the rest had scattered to
parts unknown.

This group seemed very much like the others—
striking quickly, killing and torturing without mercy,
and selling their stolen goods to the highest bidder.

Most likely the horses would go to one of the forts in
the area. Though the Southern Cheyenne had lost most
of their respected leaders to U.S. Army bullets, there
were still a number of war parties roving the area.

The army would take all the good horseflesh it could
find, no questions asked.

The afternoon wore on into evening. The traveling
was slow, due to the loss of Stick's horse and the neces-
sity for Jenny and Jessie to ride double. Windham
fought the urge to ride ahead, certain he could catch the
thieves within another full day if he were on his own.

In late evening, the sky changed. Scattered, puffy
clouds began to thin out, streaming overhead like shredded cotton.

"A wind's blowing up in them heavens," Stick said,
"a wind that blows no good."

Windham reminded him of the bad luck that had be-
fallen them the last time he had talked about the weather.
"We don't need any more of your predicting. Things are
bad enough as it is."

"Just reading the Lord's signs," Stick said. "Just
reading the signs."

Near dark, Windham led the way to the head of a

large draw. Dense clusters of willow and dogwood surrounded a gurgling spring that flowed a long stone's throw to where it joined with a stream.

The Jayhawkers had made camp in the same location, likely just before dawn that same day. They had needed some place to rest a short while and make further plans.

A small fire was built halfway down the draw, well away from the Jayhawker camp. Windham wanted no disturbance robbing him of the chance to read sign and get an idea of how many men they were following.

Stick worked with the fire and got a pan ready to warm beef and hard biscuits. Windham announced that he would go up and check out the Jayhawker camp.

"I'll go with you," Jenny said. "I want to see what you find."

"I'd sooner go alone," Windham said. "It takes me a while to read a campsite, and I don't want anything disturbed."

"How about if I just stay back at the edge of camp? I won't disturb nothing."

"Just stay here," Windham said. "Stick will fix you and Jessie something to eat."

"I'm not out here to eat," Jenny said. "I'm after those murdering Jayhawkers."

"And I'm after horses," Windham said. "You'd best let me get this done without interfering. It will be better for all of us."

Jenny began reluctantly breaking firewood over her knee. She watched Windham leave on his horse, her eyes narrowed in anger.

Windham dismounted at the edge of the Jayhawker camp. The fire had been a large one, with scraps of food scattered through the ashes. The area was littered with cigar butts and whiskey bottles. From the boot imprints, he decided that seven to eight men made up the gang, two of them quite large.

Two cards, an ace of spades and a deuce of diamonds, had fallen from a poker deck, near the charred campfire remains. Windham blew dust from them and shoved them in his pocket, vowing to locate the rest of the deck.

Just back from the campfire was a sign that Windham couldn't miss.

A cross had been made from two pieces of tree limb and tamped into the ground. Rocks and fresh soil were heaped in front of the cross, enough to signify that a man's grave might lie there.

At first Windham believed the Jayhawkers had buried one of their number. Upon close inspection, though, he saw that the cross had been left for him.

Carved in the wood were two words: FRANK WINDHAM.

Windham pulled the cross from the ground and studied it. The carving was fresh; the inside of the wood hadn't even dried yet.

As he kicked aside the rocks and loose dirt, Windham wondered who would have gone to such trouble. It had to be someone who hated him a great deal.

That could mean a lot of people.

Windham knew that, in any case, whoever had made the cross was expecting him to follow. He would have to be on the alert for ambushes.

Windham tossed the cross aside and continued to study the campsite. Nearby, he found evidence of a struggle under a tree. There were scraps of shredded clothing and strands of loose hair, long and reddish brown. He slipped some into his pocket.

Near the scene was a locket on a broken chain. The

locket, small and gold, held a picture within it, a picture of Jenny and Jessie.

The locket no doubt belonged to Jenny and Jessie's cousin, Karlie. There was no evidence that another struggle had taken place anywhere else. The Jayhawkers wouldn't have much reason to bother Aunt June, not with a young woman available.

It wasn't unusual among gangs to have women with them. It was common to violate women during raids, then kill or leave them to die, but holding hostages was extra trouble. They had to have special plans for Karlie and Aunt June.

Windham held Karlie's locket tightly and mounted his pinto. He started back for camp, feeling sick to his stomach. He was chasing men who hated him badly enough to waste their time building false graves, and who cared nothing for human virtue of any kind.

Finding them would be easy, for they wanted him to. After that, the easy part would be over. It would be a hard fight, and Windham meant to see it through to the very end.

Eight

IN CAMP, Stick and Jessie were sitting silently near the fire, eating. Jenny was pacing behind them, breaking twigs and flipping them around camp.

Stick didn't look up. Jessie looked quickly at Windham and turned back to eating.

Windham dismounted. Jenny held her gaze on Windham until his eyes met hers.

"What is it?" Windham asked.

"It took you a long time up there," she said. "How come you didn't want any of us to go with you?"

"I needed to read the signs myself, without disturbance. I explained that."

"It took you an awful long time," Jenny repeated.

"I wanted to be sure of what I saw," Windham told her. "I couldn't rush and be sure."

"Now that you've read what you want, take me up there and show me what you found."

"I'll tell you. There were seven or eight men, all heavily armed. They—"

"I don't care about that!" Jenny snapped. "Did they kill Karlie and Aunt June?"

"There's no sign that anyone was killed up there," Windham said.

"Would you tell me if they had been?"

"I'm telling you what I know," Windham said. "If they haven't killed them by now, it's likely they want to keep them alive."

"So maybe they didn't kill them," Jenny said. "Did they harm them? Did they hurt Karlie? I want you to answer me, Mr. Windham. Did they harm Karlie in any way? Could you see that they did?"

"What do you think?" Windham asked.

"I was just hoping they hadn't," Jenny said. "Just hoping."

"There's nothing we can do about it," Windham said. "I'm sorry, but we can't do a thing. All we can do is press on and find them."

Stick turned the meat and biscuits in the pan. Jessie continued to eat and stare into the fire.

Windham led his pinto out from camp, where the other horses were hobbled. After they had grazed for a while, they would be watered and brought in next to the bedrolls.

Jenny followed him, asking what he had found, wondering what would happen to Karlie and Aunt June during the coming days.

As he hobbled the pinto, Windham wished he hadn't allowed Jenny and Jessie to come along. He should have known Jenny's emotions would get the best of her. He couldn't blame her, but it would still make things difficult when the fighting started.

"We can't let them keep hurting Karlie," Jenny said. "We can't!"

"We don't have any control over what happens to them," Windham told her. "You've got to understand that."

Jenny followed Windham back to the fire, where Windham accepted a piece of beef and a biscuit from Stick. He offered the plate to Jenny.

"I don't want it," she said. "You take it."

"You can't go without food," Windham told her. "You'll need your strength."

"I don't feel much like it," Jenny said. "I feel kind of sick."

Stick and Jessie finished their meal, staring into the fire.

"Jenny, I'm sorry about all of this," Windham said, "but you've got to figure a way of handling it. If you're thinking about what happened, you can't think about what's coming up. Do you understand?"

Jenny's eyes narrowed. "You don't care a whit about Karlie, but she's my kin. I *hate* what they're doing to her. And they killed my husband. They're killing my family!"

"And they'll be killing others if we don't catch them," Windham pointed out. "We can't stop what might happen if we continue to dwell on what's already done. You understand that, don't you?"

Jenny threw a piece of firewood into the darkness. It cracked against a tree outside of camp. "I'll chase them forever," she said. "I swear I will."

Windham remembered the locket he had found, but decided against giving it to her just yet. She was still too emotional. She might decide to just ride out after them in the darkness.

Jessie turned to his sister. "Have something to eat,

Jenny. Mr. Windham's right. We've got to be strong about this. We've got to be strong in the head, and we've got to keep our bodies strong."

Jenny turned back to him. "Since when did you start taking Mr. Windham's side?"

"I didn't know we were taking sides," Jessie said. "I thought we were all in this together."

Jenny thought a moment. She walked over and took the plate from Windham and sat down. "Maybe you're right," she said to Jessie. "I guess we are all in this together."

Jessie turned to Windham. Windham winked and flashed a smile, thinking that Jenny had been right. This boy might be just twelve years old, but he certainly wasn't a boy. He wasn't a boy at all.

Stick gave Windham a plate and smiled. "I'm glad to know we're going to be working together on this," he said. "They've got us outnumbered and we need to help one another."

"I won't be no more trouble," Jenny said. "I promise. I just hate what's happening." She bowed over her plate and began to sob.

Jessie put an arm around his sister. "They'll be fine, Karlie and Aunt June. I know they will. Like Mr. Windham said, they won't likely kill them. We'll find those Jayhawkers and get them back."

"It won't be that hard finding them," Windham said. "I'll tell you all now that whoever we're after wants me to find them."

Jenny looked up and wiped her eyes. "How do you know that?"

"They made a false grave with a cross that had my name carved in it."

Stick shook his head. "That's a sick bunch. Do you know who they are?"

"I'll have to think on it," Windham said. "We'll plan to get a good rest tonight. Then we'll be in the saddle for some long stretches. They'll be looking for just me to come after them, but they'll be surprised for sure when they find out there's four of us. We'll make sure they won't know what hit them."

Nine

JUDD BARRETT spat tobacco into the dust and looked toward their backtrail. Barrett and his gang had been pushing the stolen horses hard for two days. They would continue to push them hard until they reached the hideout on the Arkansas River.

Barrett was troubled. They had just lost four head. He would send two men back after them come first light. They were worth too much to leave behind.

He stood just under a rise, in a grove of cedar, his horse grazing nearby. A hot breeze whipped his unshaven face. Light from the setting sun fired his squinting eyes, setting off the hate that burned from deep within.

Besides losing their horses, Barrett had a personal reason for watching their backtrail. Throughout the time they had been following the herd, and then after stealing the horses, the thought of Frank Windham had never left his mind.

In fact, the thought of Windham had been with him for nearly two years, ever since the death of his younger brother Kelly. Windham had gunned the younger Barrett down in northern Kansas, during a botched raid on a train of freight wagons.

Judd Barrett and his brother Kelly had come through a lot together. Three younger brothers had been killed fighting for the North, while both parents had died of fever and pneumonia.

Judd and Kelly had formed two separate gangs. In their words, they wanted to "teach the Confederates a lesson," and to "keep them from ever trying to rise again." That meant keeping the Texas cattle out of Kansas and Missouri, at any cost.

Anyone who didn't see it their way was considered the enemy, even those who had once worn a blue uniform.

With the new stockyards at Abilene, and talk of more springing up along the new railroad headed west, there was sure to be a big push of Texas cattle in the next few years. Judd and Kelly Barrett had made it their personal responsibility to keep the Southerners from moving into country now being settled and farmed.

A lot of people had called them crazy, even men who had fought alongside them. Judd and Kelly Barrett had stuck to their beliefs, though, and had vowed to take what they could from the Rebel invaders.

But Frank Windham had taken Kelly's life. Judd Barrett hadn't been the same man since.

At the time, Barrett had been leading his own gang in a stagecoach holdup near the Nebraska line, robbing and killing "Confederates who didn't know enough to stay out of Union territory."

News of his brother's death had come to him when Ben Duncan, who had ridden with Kelly, had led the straggling remainder of Kelly's gang to the hideout on the Arkansas.

Himself injured, Duncan had held his bleeding left arm, saying, "We jumped them and it would have been easy, but they had men guarding the wagons and horses. Kelly fought hard, but this one guard, this Frank Windham, came after us. He charged us on a red pinto horse, riding low like some Indian, and shot him down. Kelly didn't have a chance."

Judd Barrett had not wanted to believe his brother was dead, even when he had helped Ben Duncan unload the body from the horse.

"He'll pay, Judd," Ben Duncan had said. "This Frank Windham will get his one day. He's caused us a lot of grief."

It had been Duncan who had spotted Windham with the herd of longhorns, south of the Cimarron, less than a week back. Barrett had promised him extra pay if they killed Windham.

Barrett had always figured he'd run into Frank Windham again, sooner or later, one way or the other. The country was big and open, but Barrett had promised himself to avenge his brother's death, no matter what it took.

He would have taken Frank Windham the night they had stolen the horses, but there had been too much wind and rain. There would be another day. Soon.

As he continued to watch their backtrail, Barrett wondered what Windham had thought of the false grave. Had it scared him? Hard to tell, but it had set him to thinking, no question. It had set him to wondering.

Maybe Windham didn't know who had left the cross for him yet, but he soon would.

Barrett turned as a rider approached from behind. A small man in a beaten stovepipe hat sat awkwardly atop a large sorrel gelding, appearing as if he might fall off at any time.

Barrett angrily waved him down from the top of the rise, where he had been riding in plain sight.

Though his entire immediate family was gone, Barrett's one cousin had made it through the war and now rode with him. Of all the kin to have stayed alive, this one had seemed the most unlikely.

Coly Sterns dismounted and tied his horse to a small cedar. He scratched his unshaven face and moved next to Barrett, whacking a willow switch against his chaps. You never saw Coly Sterns without a piece of willow.

"Don't you know better than to ride along a ridge top?" Barrett asked him. "A man can see you for miles. You've lost the sense you were born with."

Coly Sterns was as small as Judd Barrett was large. His sole ambition in life was to make his cousin proud of him. More often, he filled Judd Barrett with utter discontent.

Sterns figured that his cousin Judd had always wanted to look after him. Ever since the fight in grade school, when Judd had stepped in and thrashed a kid named Lex Marshall, Coly had decided that he owed his cousin.

It didn't matter that he, Coly, had started the fight and that he couldn't finish it. He had called upon cousin Judd, who had stepped in and punched Marshall.

When Marshall was down, Sterns had pulled a small hunting knife he always carried in his pants. He had cut Lex Marshall up good.

Sterns knew that his cousin Judd had enjoyed watching him cut Marshall up. Ever since then, Sterns had cut people up, while Barrett had stood by and watched.

Coly watched Judd study their backtrail and began to whip the willow against his chaps. He held the handle of his big knife, tight in its sheath, with his free hand. He always held his knife and swatted with the switch. It made him feel powerful.

Sterns watched Barrett squint into the distance. He knew that Judd wanted the lost horses back, but he knew Judd was mainly watching for Frank Windham.

"You think Windham's back there, Judd? You figure he's trailing us?"

Barrett spat tobacco. "No doubt in my mind. Is camp made yet?"

"Yeah. The horses are all hobbled."

"What are the others doing?"

"Laying around, mostly. Playing cards and such."

"And the women?"

"They're just sitting. They just stare. That's all."

Barrett turned to Sterns. "Are you and the others leaving them be?"

"Yeah, we're not bothering them."

"You sure?"

"I wouldn't lie to you, Judd. I wouldn't."

Barrett turned back to the trail, looking through the twilight, hoping to see a rider. "I don't want them women harmed no more," he told Sterns. "I think we made a mistake last night."

"Nobody's bothering them, Judd. They're not."

"The Jacobs bunch said they wanted women fresh, not used up. They want them in good order. They'll pay us in gold. The old man told me as much. I don't want them women hurt no more."

"I know, Judd," Sterns said. "You told me plenty of times."

"Just so you remember it."

Sterns looked across the plains, envisioning himself cutting Frank Windham with his knife. He didn't even carry a gun; he had trouble hitting anything. Gunfights made him want to turn and run.

Yet if he could cut Frank Windham, it would be the best thing he had ever done in his life. Cousin Judd would care about him then.

Sterns stepped from one foot to the other, holding the knife, swatting the willow against his leg. "You bet, Judd. Let him come. We'll do him in. We'll get him."

"Calm down," Barrett said. "There's no call for dancing just yet."

Sterns frowned. "I was just trying to show I was behind you, that's all. I can see that you're worried some about Windham. He won't be no easy kill."

"Just the same, I'll get it done," Barrett said. "I'll make him sorry he ever drew a bead on Kelly."

"How do you figure to do it?" Sterns asked. "Will you let me cut him?"

"I'll know when the time comes," Barrett replied. "Just don't go badgering me about it. We've got the horses and the women to sell yet. One thing at a time."

"I didn't mean to rile you," Sterns said.

Barrett was moving for his horse. "Mount up. We're headed back to camp. I'll send you and two of the younger hands back for the horses in the morning."

"Do I have to go, Judd?"

Barrett turned. "I said you had to go. Any questions?" He untied his horse.

"What if we find Windham?" Sterns asked.

"You ain't likely to find him. He'll see you first."

"He shot the hell out of Duncan and the others back at that cattle herd," Sterns said. "I just figured you didn't want him getting any closer to us."

Barrett climbed into the saddle. "I told you I'd handle him!" he yelled. "Can't you hear? You'll go with the other two in the morning and bring those four lost horses back." He kicked his horse into a gallop.

Sterns put the willow between his teeth and struggled onto the big sorrel. He removed the whip and switched the horse, working to catch up with Barrett.

As he rode, he said under his breath, "I hope Windham's a long ways back. A long ways."

Ten

THE SUN was topping the horizon, promising heat that could boil water in a tin cup.

Windham led the way out of camp. Everyone was ready for a long, hard ride. Even Jessie, who had never complained about his arm, had a determined look to him. Stick had dressed his wound again and announced the arm was healing well.

The trail continued over uneven country. The Jayhawkers were sticking to country seldom crossed by travelers. Windham knew by now that they intended to sell the horses at one of the forts that lay to the north.

As they neared the Medicine Lodge River, Windham knew the Jayhawkers would have to make a decision soon on which fort to choose.

To the north and west lay Fort Dodge and Fort Larned. And farther yet was Fort Hays. All of these posts would be in the market for horses.

If the trail continued north, however, Windham knew they would be headed for Fort Riley.

Near noon, Stick pointed into a nearby grove of trees. "Won't you look at that! Two loose horses. And from our outfit!"

"The Jayhawkers must have lost them," Windham said. "We couldn't ask for better luck."

Stick was disappointed that one of them wasn't Jackson, but gave due account to the Lord anyway.

"The mottled gray is near wild," Windham said. "Who goes after it?"

Stick pulled a two-bit piece from his pocket. "Heads or tails?"

"Heads," Windham said.

Stick flipped the coin and caught it on the back of his hand. He showed it to Windham. "You lose."

Windham frowned. "You do that every time."

"It's the Lord's will," Stick said.

Windham fixed a noose on his lariat. "I wish we had Charlie Graham with us."

Stick and Windham approached the horses from two sides. The mottled gray stuck its nose into the air and bolted. Windham kicked his pinto into a run, his lasso ready.

The gray led Windham through the hills, dodging and turning. Windham's pinto never slowed, finally driving the gray to exhaustion.

Windham tossed the noose over the gray's neck. He had led the horse only a short distance when he heard gunfire.

Windham hobbled the gray and rode quickly toward the gunfire. Three shots sounded as he rode up next to Stick and Jessie, who had taken cover in a grove of cedars. The gunfire stopped.

"What's going on?" Windham asked.

"Three Jayhawkers showed up," Stick said. "Jenny opened fire. She hit one of them."

"How do you know they were Jayhawkers?"

"They were driving two of our horses," Stick replied. "I figure they were looking for the other two that we found. But I didn't tell Jenny to start shooting. There could be more Jayhawkers close by."

"Where's she now?" Windham asked.

Jessie spoke up, an edge to his voice. "She went after them. She's a damn fool, without a lick of sense. She won't listen to nobody."

"I'll go find her," Windham said.

There had been no more gunfire. Windham circled around toward the area where he had last heard the shooting. For a while, he couldn't see or hear anything. Then he spotted Jenny.

She was at the bottom of a draw, crouched behind Molly, her rifle leveled overside. The horse was dead.

Windham dismounted and led his pinto along the edge of the hill, watching carefully. Jenny was aiming up the hill at two men who had taken cover behind a fallen tree. When they saw Windham, the two snuck back over the hill.

Windham saw a third man, small, wearing a beaten stovepipe hat, riding a big sorrel, leading two horses. The two ran to him and mounted quickly.

Jenny ran up the hill. Windham yelled across at her, "Jenny, wait!" But Jenny was already to the top.

The three men were riding full speed along a ridge to the east. Jenny dropped to one knee and fired. The last rider toppled from the saddle.

Jenny levered another round into the barrel of her Henry rifle. The two riders quickly disappeared into a distant draw, leaving the fallen Jayhawker behind.

From the draw came two successive shots. At first,

Windham was puzzled by the gunfire. Then he realized that the Jayhawkers had likely shot the two horses they had captured. They could not drive them and hope to make a quick getaway, so they decided no one would have them.

The two remaining Jayhawkers soon appeared on the other side of the draw, riding as fast as they could. They were not driving horses ahead of them.

Jenny brought her rifle to her shoulder and fired quickly. She levered in another round and fired again, but the two riders were lost among the hills.

Windham rode to Jenny and dismounted. "Are you hurt?"

Jenny was walking away from him, toward the fallen horse. "I wish Molly would get up. But she never will."

Windham caught her. "Jenny, are you hurt at all?"

"No," Jenny replied. "But I got one of them."

"You shouldn't have gone after them, Jenny. You could have been killed."

"What's to live for?"

"What do you mean by that?"

"There's no reason for me to live. I have nothing."

"How about Jessie, for starters?"

"He doesn't need me. He can take care of himself."

"He *does* need you," Windham argued. "He thinks a lot of you, and he worries about you. He deserves better than that."

Jenny began loading bullets into her rifle. "I'm sorry if I can't please everybody all of the time, Mr. Windham. I needed to go after those men, so I did."

Windham pointed down the hill to Molly. "And it cost you a real fine horse. We can't afford to lose any more horses."

"You just caught two more, didn't you?"

"What if we hadn't caught them?"

"I don't mind walking," Jenny said. "I'll catch up to the rest of them one way or another."

Jenny started down toward Molly. Windham watched her for a time, wondering how he was going to make her understand that they needed to all be together when they started fighting. They couldn't go off individually and expect to do any good.

Jenny was headstrong beyond comparison. That was good, to a point. But if she continued to try and go after Jayhawkers on her own, she wouldn't have to worry about finding Karlie and Aunt June. She wouldn't be around to worry about anyone.

Eleven

J ENNY HAD reached Molly and was standing over her. She knelt down and stroked the dead horse's neck. Windham decided she needed time to herself.

Windham climbed onto his pinto. He rode quickly to the fallen Jayhawker and dismounted.

The thief looked well into his thirties. His eyes were open, dull and glazed over. Blood had flowed from his mouth and nose, staining his shirt. The soil under his chest was dark and wet. Jenny had shot him through the lungs.`

There were also fresh bloodstains on his shirt along his upper left arm. He had been the one Jenny had wounded earlier.

The thief's pistol had been lost. Windham stripped the remaining cartridges, .44 caliber, from the gunbelt. They would be needing all the ammunition they could get.

Windham studied the dead Jayhawker, wondering who

was leading the gang. The cross and false grave came to mind, but he still didn't have any idea who it was that so badly wanted him to die.

He couldn't waste time now wondering. He would know soon enough.

Windham rode into the draw from where the two had come. He found that he had been right about what the Jayhawkers had been shooting at.

Two fine young cow ponies lay dead at the bottom of the draw, both sturdy roan geldings. Charlie Graham had been working on them ever since the drive had started. He had intended to sell them in Abilene.

Now Charlie would never see them again. They had been hobbled and tied to a cedar tree. The Jayhawkers had killed them, each with one shot behind the ear.

Windham rode back to Jenny. She had just finished removing the saddle from Molly and had started up the other side, carrying it over her back.

Windham crossed the draw. "Hand me the saddle. I can carry it while we ride double."

"Just leave me be, Mr. Windham."

"We're losing time, Jenny."

Jenny stopped and glared up at him. "I'm not helpless, Mr. Windham. To hear you talk, you'd think I couldn't do a thing on my own."

"Some things, like chasing Jayhawkers, shouldn't be done on your own."

Jenny resumed walking. "Listen, Mr. Windham, if I see more of them and you're not around, you can bet I'll open fire again."

"Would you stop calling me Mr. Windham. My name is Frank."

"Okay, Frank. I want to gun down Jayhawkers. Do you have a problem with that?"

"Only that you might get gunned down yourself. Hand me the saddle and climb on behind me, please."

"I don't need help, Mr. Windham. Frank."

"It's not help, Jenny. It's a matter of saving time. If you want to stop those Jayhawkers and get your kin back from them, we've got to hurry."

Jenny reluctantly handed him the saddle. He swung it to the off side and slipped his boot out of the stirrup.

"I'll walk," she said.

"Climb on." Windham waited. "Please?"

Jenny planted her boot in the stirrup and let Windham pull her up by the arm. At first, she held on to the back of the saddle, but the ride uphill was causing her to slip. She wrapped her arms around Windham's middle and held herself tightly to him.

Windham liked the feel of her, warm and pleasant, even though her breathing was heavy with anger. He looked down at her hands, clasped around him, and asked if she was comfortable.

"Oh, I could just fall asleep here!" she said. "Hell no, I don't like this! I'm used to riding by myself."

"You've been riding double with Jessie. I haven't heard you complain yet."

"He's not as bossy as you," she said. "And he handles a horse better, too."

Windham eased his pinto up over the top of the ridge and down through an open park to where Stick and Jessie waited.

Jenny quickly jumped off Windham's pinto. "Can I have my saddle, please?"

Windham handed her the saddle. Jessie walked over and stuck his face in hers.

"Hey, Gunslinger Mamma! Have you shot all the Jayhawkers up yet?"

Jenny brushed by him and threw the saddle on the

ground. When he followed her, demanding an answer, she turned. "Maybe you would just as soon they had shot us up. They would have, if I hadn't opened fire."

"They were running away from us!" Jessie said. "They would have been gone except that you winged one of them."

"Well, I finished him off," Jenny said. "And I'll finish the rest of them, too."

"Why were you riding with Mr. Windham?" Jessie asked. "Where's Molly?"

Jenny turned and began walking. Jessie caught her.

"Jenny, where's Molly? What happened to her?"

"They shot her," Jenny said. "I'm sorry." Her eyes flooded with tears.

"What? She's dead?"

"Yes. I told you, the Jayhawkers killed her. They were shooting at me."

"Where is she?"

Jenny pointed. "In a draw over there. You don't want to see her."

"Why did you have to go after them?" Jessie yelled. "Look what you've done. I *hate* you!" He turned and ran a distance away, dropping to his knees in tears.

"I'll go talk to him," Stick said. "I know how he feels."

Jenny covered her face with her hands. "I've never done anything right by Jessie," she sobbed. "And now I've gone and got Molly killed. She was such a good horse."

Windham held her while she cried into his chest. She talked about how the Jayhawkers had ruined their lives, taken everything that was dear to them.

"You and Jessie have each other," Windham said. "For my money, you're both a lot to live for."

"I'm not worth anything," Jenny said. "Jessie's a fine young man. I wish I hadn't been born."

"You're wrong, Jenny," Windham told her. "You've got a lot to be proud of. I'll bet you were the best wife a man could ask for."

Jenny looked up at him. "Why would you say that?"

"It just seems that way to me," Windham said. He let her go and climbed back on his pinto. "I caught the gray and hobbled her a short ways from here. I'm going to bring her back. Promise me you won't go anywhere. Promise me you won't leave."

"Where would I go?"

"Just promise me, Jenny."

"I promise. I'll stay right here."

"Tell Stick and Jessie where I went," Windham said. He turned his pinto.

Jenny stopped him. "Mr. Windham, that was a nice thing to tell me. I mean, about being a good wife. Thank you, Mr. Windham."

"It's Frank."

"Thank you, Frank. I appreciate your kind words. Thank you."

"I meant it, Jenny," he said. "You're a fine woman. You have a good future ahead of you. Remember that. There are people who care about you. Don't take any more chances."

"I'm sorry, Frank. I'm sorry for what I did."

"Just don't do it again, Jenny. None of us want to see anything happen to you."

"You're serious about that, aren't you?" Jenny said.

"Yes, very serious. Let's work together, like Jessie suggested. Is that a deal?"

"It's a deal, Frank. I promise this time. I'll go bury that Jayhawker I shot, because I said I wanted to bury them all. Then we'll go on, and I'll never act crazy again."

Twelve

WINDHAM RETURNED with the gray mare. Jenny had buried the dead Jayhawker, no doubt in a shallow grave, and was facing her brother, her hands on her hips.

Stick was now talking with Jessie and Jenny together, helping them iron out their feelings about losing Molly. From Windham's position, it didn't appear that he was doing too well.

Windham decided he would ride the gray mare, to work out the wildness. He was loosening the saddle on his pinto when Jenny came up to him.

"Are you planning on riding the gray?" she asked.

"Until the kinks are worked out, yes," he replied.

"I'm responsible for what happened to Molly," Jenny said. "I'll take the gray mare."

"She's got a wild streak."

"I know that. I could see it the first thing."

"Have you worked with horses?"

"I'll show you how much I know about horses," she said. "I'll put *my* saddle on her."

"Jenny, you promised not to lose your head again," Windham reminded her.

"I know what I'm doing this time," Jenny said. She winked. "I *always* know what I'm doing. It just doesn't seem that way to folks watching."

Windham stepped back and Jenny took the mare. She led the horse over to where her saddle lay on the ground.

Stick joined Windham. He pointed back to where he had left Jessie, sitting on the ground chewing a blade of grass.

"That Jessie has had to grow up fast," Stick said. "I had a good talk with him. He hasn't had an easy life."

"And if the last few days are any indication," Windham said, "the rest of his life won't ease up any. What does he do to make it easier for himself?"

"He holds on to the same things I did at his age," Stick said. "He had a pet dog when he was little. And a couple of good horses. Of course, they lost Molly."

"How does he feel toward Jenny now?" Windham asked.

"It's going to take some time," Stick replied. "He knows how she feels toward those Jayhawkers, but he can't forgive her yet for getting Molly killed."

Windham pointed to where Jenny was saddling the gray mare. "She says she's responsible for all this and that she'll ride that mare."

Stick shook his head. "She's awful hard on herself. You won't make her do it, will you, Frank?"

"I can't make her do anything," Windham said. "And I can't make her *not* do anything, either. She's determined."

"But that horse could hurt her."

"I told her that."

"She won't stay on it."

"I told her that, too. She told me to just watch."

"Maybe we can get Jessie to talk with her," Stick said. "She promised him she would listen from now on."

Stick and Windham walked over to where Jessie chewed on his blade of grass, his eye on his sister and the gray mare.

"Jessie," Stick began, "do you think you can help us stop Jenny from getting on that mare?"

Jessie spoke through the grass. "Why would I want to do that?"

"She could get hurt, that's why," Stick said. "That wouldn't be good."

"I'm not going to say nothing to her," Jessie said. "She can take care of herself."

Windham knelt down beside Jessie. "Are you that angry at your sister, that you would want to see her get hurt?"

"It doesn't matter whether I'm that angry at her or not. She's not about to get hurt."

"Is she that good with horses?" Windham asked.

"You'll see," Jessie said.

Jenny tightened the cinch. The mare's ears were flat against her head. Jenny jumped quickly into the saddle, pulling up on the reins.

The mare began to crow-hop, bouncing stiff-legged. Jenny spurred the mare, her knees in tight.

The mare squealed in anger and began to buck, jumping and kicking in a tight circle. Jenny, one arm flying high above her head, stayed on like she was glued.

Jessie turned to Stick and Windham. "What did I tell

you? I'd like to see her hit the ground. But she won't. She's a bronc-bustin' wild woman, she is."

"Where did she learn to ride like that?" Stick asked.

"She's broke horses since she was a little girl," Jessie replied. "It's pretty hard to find a horse that she can't ride."

The gray mare stopped bucking. Jenny spurred her into a trot and then a gallop, riding up and down the surrounding hills. She returned with the mare, smiling. "We ready to ride on?"

"Time's a-wasting," Windham said, mounting his pinto. "We've got Jayhawkers to catch."

Thirteen

JUDD BARRETT sat his horse atop a hill, looking to the south. The sun was falling, filling the hills with shadows.

A few miles ahead, the hills broke out into open country. The others were driving the horses toward a night bedding ground. Behind, Coly and the other two had to be lost somewhere.

Coly had been gone a day and a half. Barrett was troubled. He didn't want to leave his cousin behind and he couldn't afford to lose the time waiting for him.

Barrett knew he should have sent at least one more man along, possibly two. Coly wasn't capable of doing any job on his own, and he couldn't manage men very well.

But Barrett had wanted to give Coly a chance to prove himself to the others. Everyone thought he was excess baggage. Barrett had hoped that if Coly could lead the other two and bring back the four lost horses, he might gain some respect.

He should have known that Coly couldn't do anything to gain respect from the others. Especially Ben Duncan.

He should have sent Ben Duncan instead. Duncan, who had ridden with his brother Kelly and his gang, was dependable and made good decisions. Duncan had hung with his brother, fighting Frank Windham to the last. Duncan could lead men a lot better than Coly.

The trouble was, Duncan and Coly had a continual feud, one that could easily end in blood. If it hadn't been for Duncan's loyalty to Kelly, he might have let him go long before. He couldn't afford to have any wrangling in camp. It made for unrest among the men.

Barrett fidgeted in his saddle. Coly should have returned with the horses way before now. Now he hoped that, if nothing else, Coly and the other two would just return.

Barrett hadn't counted on losing four men back at the cattle herd. Now he was very shorthanded. He had Frank Windham to thank for that. As always, Windham was causing him considerable trouble.

In addition, he knew Frank Windham was trailing them, likely gaining a lot of ground every day. He wondered if Windham hadn't found Coly and the other two.

As he fretted, Barrett noticed someone approaching, riding a sleek red stallion. Del Brice, his right-hand man from the main hideout, reined in, out of breath.

"What the hell you doing here?" Barrett asked. "You're supposed to be back on the river."

Brice, a tall Union veteran in his late twenties, had spent his whole life fighting. He had been with Kelly's gang also, and had joined Barrett's bunch with Ben Duncan.

Brice now spent his time overseeing the main hideout when Barrett was out raiding. He was having trouble finding words to tell Barrett what had happened at the main hideout.

"I asked you what you're doing here!" Barrett yelled. "I want to know. Now!"

"We've had bad trouble, Judd," Brice managed. "We lost all the horses to renegade Cheyenne."

"What? All of them?"

"Every last one. I'd just got done branding them. I got out, along with Jonesy and Milt. They got Riley, though. We could hear him a-screaming. I still can't get it out of my head."

Barrett slammed a fist against the saddle horn. "Damn! I've got enough trouble as it is. We lost all the horses?"

"All twenty head, slick as you please," Brice said. "Nothing we could do about it."

Barrett was beside himself. He had planned to bring in the horses from the trail herd, change the brands, and sell them along with the horses they had collected at the main hideout. He had hoped to ride away from Fort Dodge with a good load of gold coin.

"Why didn't you stop them Cheyenne?" Barrett asked.

"Judd, we couldn't," Brice said. "There was way too many. Must of been thirty or forty. We didn't stand a chance."

"I thought them damn soldiers was protecting us citizens!" Barrett yelled. "I thought they stopped them Cheyenne."

"I told you there was renegades around," Brice said.

"They killed a bunch of them, but you ain't going to stop them all. That ain't going to happen."

"Them damn soldiers!" Barrett went on. "They ain't doing their job."

"Them Cheyenne have been around for a spell," Brice said. "We knew it. I told you we'd ought to sell those horses we had before you took off south after the trail herds. Didn't I?"

"I don't want to hear about it. How did you find me, anyway?"

"We all three rode down here looking for you. We've been riding steady for three days. We just found Duncan and the others a piece back, bedded for the night. I figured I'd find you and let you know what happened. I didn't want you to get riled when you got to camp and saw us there."

"What, you don't think I'm riled now?" Barrett snarled.

"Yeah, I figure you are, Judd," Brice said. "But it wasn't our fault. Them Cheyenne have been around, you know. We seen the buffalo dust. You remember that."

"I told you, I don't want to hear no more about it," Barrett said. "What's done is done. We've got other troubles now."

"I hear Coly took after some horses you lost."

"He ain't back yet. I don't like any of this."

"Maybe we'd ought to go and find him and the other two," Brice suggested.

"It's too near dark," Barrett said. "We'll head up to where they've bedded the horses. If Coly ain't back come first light, we'll go looking, you and I."

Brice pointed out across the plains to the west, into the fading crimson. "You know, Judd, there's a big horse ranch out that way. The JY outfit. Maybe we'd ought to hit them and get some more horses."

"That's a far piece out," Barrett said. "Off the trail back to the river."

"Hell, there ain't nothing back at the river," Brice pointed out. "We need a good amount of horses to sell at Fort Dodge. What you got from that herd ain't near enough, is it?"

"We could use more, at that," Barrett said. "But first we've got to find Coly."

"I can see pretty good in the dark, Judd. Maybe I should go now."

"Nobody's going anywhere unless I say. And when we do, it'll be in bunches."

"I figure you're talking about Frank Windham," Brice said. "Duncan said Windham shot everybody up at the trail herd, and that he's likely on your trail. You figure he got Coly?"

"I don't want to hear that!" Barrett yelled. "I figure Coly can get away from him. Hell, Coly'd run if he saw him within four miles."

Brice laughed. "I reckon that's true enough. Coly never could hold his ground. Probably better that way where Frank Windham's concerned."

"Well, Frank Windham ain't long for this world," Barrett said. "I'm tired of hearing about him and I don't figure to worry about him any longer. He's done me wrong and I aim to make him pay."

Barrett kicked his horse into a gallop. Brice followed, taking a quick glance back.

Talking about Frank Windham made him nervous. He had seen Windham fight during the botched raid on the freight wagons. He had seen Windham gun Kelly down and wound Ben Duncan in the arm. He had been lucky that Windham hadn't gotten to him as well.

Now he was a lot closer to Frank Windham than he had ever thought he'd be again. He didn't like it at all. If he had his druthers, he'd ride back to the Arkansas River and stay in the hideout, Cheyenne or no Cheyenne. There were a lot of things he'd sooner face than Frank Windham.

Fourteen

'M TELLING you, there's more of them than just Frank Windham. You'd better believe me."

Coly Sterns was pacing back and forth in front of the fire, switching a piece of willow against his chaps. Judd Barrett scratched his unshaven face, listening intently, while the others looked on.

"That woman shot at us like she'd handled a rifle all her life," Sterns continued. "We dropped her horse, but we still couldn't get anywhere near her. And then Windham showed up."

Barrett had been glad to see Coly ride into camp, even if he had scared everyone and had nearly gotten himself shot in the dark. But now he wished Coly would let it go and allow everyone to get some rest.

"Windham just sat there on that pinto of his, getting ready to come at us," Sterns said.

"Maybe he was riding alone and just came upon you," Barrett suggested. "Maybe he just showed up."

Sterns slapped the willow against his chaps. "Have it your way, Judd, but I'm telling you that Windham was with them. I figure they've been riding together all along. Them and that kid. And the slave. I know Windham's taken a slave along. I saw him."

"Windham don't take to slaves," Barrett said. "What's the matter with you? He wouldn't have no slave with him."

Del Brice sat down and drew his knees up. No matter how important Coly Sterns thought he was, Brice was too tired to listen. He lowered his head and fell asleep.

Ben Duncan stood with his thumbs resting on his gunbelt. He had been the one to bring the body of Kelly Barrett back to his brother Judd. Nothing in the gang had been the same since.

Duncan believed he had as much against Frank Windham as anybody. Kelly Barrett had been his best friend. In addition, he would never have full use of his left arm, due to a bullet from Windham.

Nearly thirty, Duncan felt he had twice as much sense as anyone else in the gang, including Judd Barrett. Working for Kelly had been a lot better. And he had not had to put up with the likes of Coly Sterns.

Nearly as large as Barrett, Duncan had expressed his view of Sterns aloud several times. "He's worthless," he had said during a card game. "Someone ought to just knock him in the head and toss him off a cliff." There had been some snickers, but no one had wanted to go against Judd Barrett.

At this point, Duncan didn't care who was with him. He wanted no more time wasted because of Coly Sterns. Everyone needed rest, especially if they were going to head west and raid the big JY horse outfit.

Duncan knew Windham didn't believe in slaves. Besides, a slave wasn't allowed to carry a big Colt and shoot it whenever he wanted. Coly Sterns should have known that; but Coly Sterns was the biggest fool ever born.

"Coly, let it go," Duncan said. "We'll take it up in the morning."

"I ain't talking to you, Duncan," Sterns spat. "I'm talking to Judd. And I know Windham's got a slave with him. We'd ought to make him pay for that kind of thing."

"You can be sure he's no slave," Barrett said. "If you remember, we saw him trailing beeves with the rest of the drovers. He's a working cowhand. I don't know why he'd be with Windham."

"Well he was," Sterns said. "He had one of the horses we lost. I don't know where the gray mare got to, the wild one. But we wound up with just two of them."

"You still ain't given me a good reason why you shot them," Barrett said.

Sterns whipped himself harder. "I told you, Judd, Windham would've caught us if we'd tried to drive them. I didn't want him to have them, so I shot them. I thought I did good."

"You didn't do good at all," Barrett said. "I told you to go and get those four horses. Instead, you come back without one of the men and without any of the horses. I can't send you nowhere but you don't mess it all up."

"Coly's good at messing things up," Duncan said. "He won't listen to reason of any kind. But I guess there's nothing new about that."

Sterns turned to face Duncan. "I thought I told you to stay out of this."

"You *thought*, Coly. You can't think."

"What did you say?"

"You know what I said, Coly. You couldn't think your way out of a shirt. You're the biggest headache of this whole outfit. Your mother should have knocked you in the head and saved everyone a lot of trouble."

Sterns put his hand on his knife handle. "I'd ought to gut you, Duncan."

"Come ahead, Coly," Duncan said. "I've never killed a worm your size before."

"That's enough, both of you!" Barrett yelled. "I told you before, there'll be no fighting in my outfit. I want that understood!"

Sterns glared. Ben Duncan spat and laughed.

"Duncan, I don't want you pushing Coly," Barrett said. "We mean to be at that horse ranch by late tomorrow. We can't be working together if we're at odds. Do you hear me?"

Duncan kicked at the dirt.

"Duncan?" Barrett said. "I asked you if you understood me."

Duncan looked up. "Yeah, Judd, I understand you."

Duncan was angry about a lot of things within the gang. He was the only survivor of the group left behind when the horses had been stolen from the herd. He hadn't liked what had happened that night.

Their job had been to kill the wrangler and stop anyone who came after them. Duncan had argued just to get out with the horses and set up an ambush along the river for those who tried to follow. He hadn't wanted to meet Frank Windham again.

But Barrett had insisted that five men stay back. Duncan had been ordered to command the men.

They had gotten the wrangler, and then the Negro and Frank Windham had come after them. Duncan knew he would have died himself, had he not gotten a good lead on Windham.

After the horse raid on the herd, Duncan had sworn he would never get himself into a mess like that again. He had seen about enough of Judd Barrett and Coly Sterns. Duncan couldn't see how the likes of Barrett and Sterns could manage to keep a gang together for very long.

Duncan felt that if he had anything to say about it, neither Barrett nor Sterns would be around much longer.

Duncan stayed with Barrett's gang only because he believed that, in time, he would become its leader.

Another Jayhawker, Dirk Markham, felt just as much contempt for Barrett and Sterns. Also in his twenties, he was a loner who couldn't care less about any of the gang members.

Exceptionally good with horses, Markham was the sole reason the herd hadn't scattered yet. Barrett realized what he had in Markham and allowed him more leeway than any of the others, including his cousin Sterns.

Markham also fancied himself a card shark. They had pulled from a deck the first night out to see who got the young woman first. Through sleight of hand, Markham had drawn the highest card.

An angered Coly Sterns had challenged him. In the scuffle, he had lost the ace of spades and the deuce of diamonds from the deck. He had discovered it along the trail the following day.

After finishing with the girl, Markham had convinced Barrett to disallow the others their turns, saying that the girl would be ruined and not good for sale to the Jacobs bunch. She was too high strung, he had told Barrett, and would likely lose her mind with continued use.

Barrett had agreed with him, after first taking his own turn.

After that, no one but Judd Barrett cared even a little

bit for Dirk Markham. It didn't bother Markham: Judd Barrett was the law in this Jayhawker camp. No one else mattered.

Markham knew that Barrett needed him to get the horses to the hideout and on to Fort Dodge. Barrett paid him well to keep the horses under control.

Markham watched Sterns glare at Duncan, squeezing the handle of his knife. He had to agree with Duncan: Coly Sterns was as worthless as they come. It would be better to just put him to sleep. Permanently.

But Judd Barrett wanted Sterns around. Barrett liked to watch him carve people up. Markham could barely stomach the two, but realized that Barrett had established himself as the gang leader. He had ties that could mean a lot of money to someone who knew horses.

And Dirk Markham knew horses. The more horses he handled, the more he liked it. He would just bide his time and keep making money from Judd Barrett. Nothing else mattered.

Fifteen

DEL BRICE had fallen over on his side and was sleeping soundly. Others of the gang had gone back to their bedrolls. They all knew how tough the following day would be. Barrett had talked about a hard ride to the west, to steal more horses.

They were all too tired to care about losing horses to the Cheyenne. They now worried about how much extra time it was going to take stealing more horses. It would be a lot easier to just drive the horses they had back to the hideout, change the brands, and sell them to the army.

But Judd Barrett was a greedy man. Losing his brother had not changed that; it had only changed his will to live. Many of the gang members now wondered if he didn't harbor a death wish.

Taking more time to reach the hideout was certainly a death wish, especially with Frank Windham catching up.

Coly Sterns hadn't cared about the news of losing the

horses. He was pacing again, whipping himself with the willow, talking again about the woman.

"It wouldn't matter if she was an ordinary female," he was saying, "but she's not. She can ride and she can handle a rifle. That changes the odds, Judd. It ain't good."

Barrett rubbed his face. "Do you figure to quit on me, Coly?"

"No, Judd, I didn't mean that. I don't like the idea of the woman with the rifle, though." He pointed over to Aunt June and Karlie. They were both sitting with their backs to a tree, tied hand and foot. "That big woman over there told us she'd come. She warned us. We didn't believe her, though. That woman and Windham, together . . . it just ain't good, Judd."

Judd Barrett had a reason for listening to his cousin's ramblings. Coly was worthless when he was upset. He was fidgety and he was hard to be around.

Barrett wanted Coly as peaceful as he could have him. He didn't like Coly keeping everyone on edge.

Barrett had found that if he let Coly talk about it long enough, Coly would settle himself down. He could tell Coly a lot of things that would help. Sometimes it was hard to deal with, though, and it seemed as if Coly was more trouble than he was worth.

He would never get rid of Coly, however. He enjoyed seeing Coly use his knife on people. He enjoyed it a lot. Coly knew how to please him. He had to keep Coly contented.

Sterns was pointing to the big woman. "I hate her. I hate her for having that girl come after us with Windham. I hate her!"

Aunt June sat glaring. Yes, she had said Jenny would be coming. It had started right after the little man with the stovepipe hat had gutted her husband. Not batting an eye, she had said there would be blood for blood to pay.

"You go ahead and cut him up," she had told Sterns. "You'll die when my niece comes along. There aren't enough of you to stop her."

She knew how much it bothered the terrible little man in the stovepipe hat. He had beaten her many times with his willow, but she had never stopped taunting him about Jenny.

"She'll shoot you down, you little bastard!" June would say. "You'll get one right in the head."

Now she knew for certain that Jenny had come to find her and Karlie. That was good to know.

June Marker was a strongly built woman, not tall, but stout. In her mid fifties, she had come to Missouri on a flatboat as a child. Her parents had migrated to Texas, where her father had worked for a large rancher.

She had married a man from Virginia who had come west to make a new life for himself. They had raised a single child, Karlie, with only the war breaking into their lives. June had hoped the end of the war would bring better times. She had been wrong.

The Jayhawkers had come in the night and had ruined everything, including her daughter. Now Karlie just stared into space. She wouldn't eat and barely took water.

June was growing more worried. Though they hadn't touched her since the first night, Karlie acted as if she wanted to die.

The terrible little man with the knife and the stovepipe hat continued to talk about Jenny. The more he talked about her, the more June liked it. It gave June a sense of hope. From now on she would cause Sterns as much trouble as she could.

June had been waiting for death when they had cut her husband. She hadn't cared; there was nothing to live for. She knew they would take Karlie. She knew what they would do to her.

Then June had been surprised when they had taken her as well. Barrett had tied her hands behind her and had forced her up on a horse.

What did they want with a big, middle-aged woman? She had yet to figure that out.

Now Jenny was coming for certain. And she had killed one of the Jayhawkers.

She knew nothing about this Frank Windham, only what she had heard from the Jayhawkers talking among themselves. She knew that he was a hired gunfighter for a trail herd that had lost their horses. If he was half as good a shot as Jenny, he must be very good.

Sterns continued to wail. Barrett straightened himself up and yelled, "Stop that crying and come over here!" He wanted to keep Coly content, but there was a limit to a man's patience.

Sterns balked. "What do you want, Judd?"

"I said come over here, Coly."

Sterns walked hesitantly. When he stopped in front of Barrett, his eyes were down.

Barrett grabbed the willow switch and began slapping Sterns in the face and head. Sterns brought his hands up.

"Don't, Judd," Sterns whined. "Why you hitting me?"

"I don't like it that you've turned yellow on me, Coly," Barrett replied, stopping to catch his breath. "I don't want to hear you talking like this again. Ever."

Sterns was on his knees, covering his face. "I won't, Judd. I won't. I promise."

Barrett tossed the switch aside. Sterns came to his feet and grabbed the switch. He walked in a circle, whipping the willow around, as if swatting at flies.

Suddenly, Sterns started for Aunt June. He began swatting her with the willow.

Sterns pulled his knife. Barrett grabbed his arm from behind. He took the knife and pointed it in Sterns' face.

"I thought I told you to leave that woman alone."

"It's her fault they've all come after us."

"I don't care. I want you to quit whupping her. She's swollen up so much now that Jacobs might not want her."

"He likely wouldn't have wanted her, anyways," Sterns protested.

"I'll be the judge of that!" Barrett yelled. "You do as I say. Understand?"

"Yeah, Judd. I understand."

Barrett's eyes were wide with anger. "I don't want to have to talk to you again about this. We've got to stay on Jacobs' good side. Next time I'll take your knife and let the woman whup you good."

Aunt June smiled. Now she knew why Barrett wanted her alive. She hoped Jenny and this Frank Windham caught up before they met Jacobs.

And she knew that she could do anything she wanted to Coly Sterns, just as long as Judd Barrett was nearby. She would take advantage of that. Her smile became a laugh.

Her laughter was drowned out by Ben Duncan. Dirk Markham began laughing as well and the other Jayhawkers joined in.

"Crawl in a hole, Coly," Duncan said. "And don't come out."

"Quit badgerin' him, I said!" Barrett roared.

The laughing stopped, all except Duncan.

Judd Barrett glared. "You hear me, Duncan?"

"Yeah, yeah. I hear you." Duncan turned his back and spat, then began snickering.

Coly Sterns took his knife back from Barrett. He gripped it tightly, glaring at Duncan.

"I hate him, too," he told Barrett. He was pointing the knife. "I'm going to cut Duncan. Soon. I will."

"We've got horses to get and horses to sell," Barrett said. "We need everyone to get it done."

Sterns walked out of the light of the fire and sat down by himself in the shadows. He pulled a whetstone from his pocket and began to sharpen the knife. He stared back into camp at Duncan, who was joking with the others.

Sterns began to breathe heavily. In his mind he could see Duncan, tied out on the ground in front of him, his stomach exposed.

A surge of glee ran through Sterns as he saw himself ramming the blade of his knife into Duncan's stomach, ripping upward.

Now Sterns began to laugh. No one could hear him, but he was satisfied. He was licking his fingers of the make-believe blood, licking and slurping, as if it were real.

He sheathed his knife and promised himself that before long he would make it real. Very real.

Sixteen

DON'T need no sleep," Jessie was saying, his eyes closed. "I can't sleep. Don't let them come. Don't let them come!"

Jenny, who was sleeping beside her brother, leaned over and caught him as he awakened and sat up.

"It's just a dream," she said. "Just a bad dream. Go back to sleep."

Jessie held his breath. A nearly full moon had all but crossed the sky. Outside of camp, the crickets were noisy.

"Where are we?" Jessie asked.

"We're after the Jayhawkers, Jessie. You remember. Everything's all right."

The moon shone on Jessie's troubled face. He groaned. "I keep seeing them coming," he said. "I can't make them go away."

"Just try to relax," Jenny said. "You need the rest. We're going to be starting out again soon."

Jessie looked around. "Where's Mr. Windham?"

Jenny pointed. "He's over there. See him, sitting up, oiling his guns?"

Jessie peered through the darkness. Satisfied, he took a deep breath and lay back down. He put himself to sleep saying, "Mr. Windham will get them. Mr. Windham will get them all."

Jenny got out of her bedroll and walked over to Windham. She sat down and rubbed her tired eyes.

Windham pulled a cleaning rod through the barrel of his rifle. "Why are you up?"

"I don't feel like sleeping."

"You'd better take your own advice and go back to bed. We're going to be riding hard again come first light."

"I can't rest, knowing Jessie's afraid like that," Jenny said. "He can't stop having nightmares."

"He's been through a lot. Too much. I wish now that I hadn't shot at you two. I've just made it worse for him."

"We were out to kill both of you," Jenny said. "You didn't have any choice, if you wanted to stay alive."

Windham began loading cartridges into his rifle. "It can't be changed, I realize that, but I wish we hadn't met the way we did."

"He doesn't hold it against you," Jenny said. "In fact, he feels safe with you."

Windham set the rifle down and began cleaning the pistol. "That's a tall order. I don't know how much safety I can provide out here. We're after some vicious men. I still can't justify taking you and Jessie along."

"Why? Because I'm a woman?"

"No. You shoot as well as any man. I told you before, Jessie's too young to die."

"I'm taking responsibility for him," Jenny said. "I'm the one who insisted that we come with you. It wasn't up to you."

"Sure it was. I could have told you no."

"And you think I would have listened? No, Frank. We would have tailed along behind you anyway. You know that."

"I still worry that he'll be in the wrong place when the shooting starts."

"He won't die," Jenny insisted. "I'll be watching out for him. Stick is very protective. And I know you care about him. How could anything happen to him?"

Windham had removed the cylinder from his Colt and was cleaning the barrel. "It wouldn't be so hard if he would stay back when we find them. I don't think he will."

"What do you mean, Frank? He's not fool enough to throw himself in front of their gun sights."

"Maybe not," Windham said. "But he wants to help out. He wants to learn Indian ways and help stop the Jayhawkers. You've heard him talking, Jenny. He wants to be in the middle of this. It worries me."

"Let me ask you something, Frank," Jenny said. "Can you remember when you were his age?"

"Very well. I was living with the Cheyenne."

"And I suppose you stayed in camp and cooked with the women."

"No. I was learning to hunt, and how to be a warrior."

"Did they take you on war parties?"

"No. I wasn't old enough."

"But you wanted to go, didn't you Frank? You wanted to be with them. Tell me, honestly, didn't you?"

"Well, yes, I did," Windham said. "But the difference is, they wouldn't let me go. They don't take boys along to war, not until they think you're ready."

"Did you think you were ready?"

"I suppose so."

"Of course you did. And maybe you were. If you would have been asked, you would have gone, wouldn't you?"

"Fine, Jenny, you've made your point," Windham said, oiling his holster. "That still doesn't make it easier for me to have him along. I wouldn't want to see him hurt any more—physically or emotionally."

"I understand," Jenny said. "I can see why he feels safe with you, and trusts you. You're the first man who's ever shown him that you care about him."

Windham was peering into the east. "You've lost your chance to get some more rest. Better get ready to saddle your horse."

Jenny studied Windham's face. The light of dawn showed an eagerness in his eyes.

"I thought I was determined," she said. "But you're like some wolf. You can't wait to get on the hunt."

"It's my job," Windham said. "It's what I know."

"This is all you've ever done?"

"I'm no farmer."

"How do you do it, Frank?" she asked. "I mean, how can you live your entire life this way?"

"I don't have a lot of choice," Windham said, sliding his Colt into its holster. "Settling down isn't something I can do. It just won't happen."

"Have you ever tried?"

"Oh, I guess so. But there's something in my blood now. I can't explain it. Once you've lived with the Indians, your life changes."

"Are you saying that you can't stay away from danger?"

Windham smiled. "Yes, I suppose. Something like that. I think you're the same way."

"No," Jenny said. "I don't like being shot at."

"But you do like to challenge a strong horse," Windham said. "You'd get on a wild bronc any time of the day or night."

"I suppose you're right," Jenny said. "I won't argue that one. But it's not the same as being shot at."

"It's not a lot different," Windham said. "You're gambling that you won't get bucked off. Maybe you win most of the time, but there's always that one horse that puts you off. You could get hurt bad. That's the risk. It gets inside you. You're challenged by that. Tell me I'm wrong."

Jenny smiled. "I wouldn't want to get hurt. That would be bad."

"But it's worth the risk, just to test yourself on the horse," Windham said. "Am I right?"

"So, you're right," Jenny said. "But you still didn't win the argument."

"Oh, I know that," Windham said, rising to his feet. "I certainly know that. Roust your brother up and we'll get going."

Jenny watched Windham walk to where the horses were picketed, wondering how a man so forceful in his ways could, at times, seem so gentle.

She noticed that Jessie was awake and sitting up, pointing out toward Windham. Stick was standing near him, nodding at something he was saying.

Jenny knew that Jessie was talking about Windham and how he was going to lead them to the Jayhawkers. He could even be telling Stick that they didn't have to worry, that Windham would make sure everyone was safe.

Jenny grabbed her saddle and started toward the horses, knowing that Jessie was right: if Frank Windham said he would watch out for you, there was nothing that would stop him from doing just that. No one could ever feel safer.

Seventeen

BARRETT WATCHED his men get ready to ride. He had been holding something inside him for a long time, and it was about to burst out.

But he couldn't allow himself to give away what he believed would happen very soon. The way he had planned it, those who now rode with him would soon be dead.

Before going on the raid, he had told the Jacobs bunch to meet him at the hideout at the change of the moon. His plan had been to have the women and horses all in one place. That would make it easy to take care of things the way he saw fit, and have the Jacobs bunch there to help him.

Barrett had decided he would then get rid of everyone but Coly. All the others would fall. Every one of them.

Barrett had known for some time that his gang was on its last legs. There were too many things going wrong, too much unrest. Too many of the others were wondering if they couldn't lead better than he. It was a dangerous situation for him.

He had seen this coming for some time, well before the raid. With the series of events that had taken place over the past few days, everything had gone downhill. It was now only a matter of time until the gang self-destructed.

From the beginning of the raid, Barrett had gotten little sleep. He hadn't planned on losing four of his men right away, and he hadn't planned on renegade Cheyenne taking the horses at the hideout, and killing two more. He now wondered if the Jacobs bunch had run into the Indians.

His plans with Jacobs' men had been well laid out; they were all too eager to help. The problem now was how to handle things until they reached the hideout.

Killing the troublemakers wouldn't solve anything. There were too many against him now. Earlier, he might have gotten the younger men to side with him. Not now.

Besides, he must use them for just a while longer. With the horses from the herd, and those he expected to get from the JY, he needed every hand.

But after they reached the hideout, everything would be different.

He didn't need anyone he had in his bunch. The Jacobs bunch had a much better wrangler than Dirk Markham. Sure, Markham thought he was irreplaceable, but what did he know?

And Ben Duncan? His trust in Duncan had collapsed entirely on this trip. Maybe Duncan had fought alongside Kelly, but he had proved his hate for Coly and his disregard for everyone else.

Del Brice hadn't ever held up his end. He was always complaining and looking for the worst to happen. He had probably fallen asleep at the main camp and just let the Cheyenne waltz off with the horses.

As for the others, they were young and inexperienced. They didn't know how to handle themselves in a fight, and you couldn't teach them anything. They thought they already knew it all. They were more of a liability than an asset. Best to get rid of them all.

Barrett was proud of himself. Joining with the Jacobs gang was going to be a smart move. Jacobs' men had even less tolerance for Rebels than he did. He and Coly would become a part of a solid outfit and there wouldn't be anyone badgering Coly any longer.

Barrett dreamed how it would be: he and Coly would ride with the Jacobs bunch, he in charge of raiding for horses while Jacobs and his men continued to rob stagecoaches and freight wagons.

Together they would control the area in central and eastern Kansas, as well as southern Nebraska.

But first there remained the biggest problem of all: Frank Windham.

Barrett was anxious to settle the score with Windham. But he must go about it the right way. Windham would be a hard kill, a very hard kill. It would be better to get him back to the hideout and have Jacobs' men help out.

Barrett climbed into the saddle and gathered his men. "We're headed west," he told them. "We're going after horses over on the JY spread. I know you all figured we'd go. I'm just making it official."

Ben Duncan spoke up. "I don't think it's a good idea. It's out of our way. A lot out of our way."

Del Brice added, "And what if they have a lot of men there? Maybe we won't get any horses at all."

"I didn't ask anyone what they thought!" Barrett shouted. "I said we're all going. It's going to be a hard ride. We'll stop for water, nothing else."

June Marker, who was tied to her saddle, said, "You can't run far enough to get away from my niece."

"Why don't we just shoot her and get it over with," Duncan said. "There's no need to put up with that."

"I told you why we're keeping these women," Barrett said. "I don't want to hear any more about it."

Dirk Markham spoke up. "I haven't figured out why we need to cater to the Jacobs bunch. They work way north of us. What do we need to bring them women for?"

"I told you," Barrett replied, "they're willing to swap horses for them. We're in this thing for horses, remember?"

"What if the Cheyenne got their horses, too," Markham asked. "Then what?"

"That's not the way it is," Barrett said. "I don't want to hear any more about it. Now, let's quit wasting time and ride out of here."

Barrett kicked his horse into a gallop. The rest began pushing horses. June and Karlie's horses were each led by one of the Jayhawkers.

When he was certain that Barrett was far enough ahead not to see, Ben Duncan rode up next to Dirk Markham.

"What do you figure is wrong with Barrett?" he asked. "He's not thinking straight."

"He hasn't been thinking straight for some time," Markham said. "I'm getting sick of it."

"You figure on quitting?"

"I don't know if telling you what I think is such a good idea," Markham said. "After all, you and Kelly were pretty close."

"That was me and Kelly," Duncan said. "I don't share the same feelings for Judd. I don't figure to be taking orders from him much longer."

"Are you saying you're quitting?" Markham asked.

Duncan leaned over. "I've been holding this to myself until now. I aim to start a gang of my own."

"That so?" Markham said. "Who do you figure to have follow you."

"I'm asking you, for starters," Duncan replied. "We'd be after horses. No women for some other gang. That's crazy. We'd use who we wanted along the way and leave them behind. No blood feuds with ex-Yankees from the war. There'd be no time for any of that. Just stealing horses and selling them. What do you say?"

"I'd have to know a lot more," Markham said. "When do you aim to do this?"

"Just as soon as we sell the horses. If I can get you to come in with me, I figure most of the others will come along. Everybody but Coly."

"Don't you figure Barrett and Coly will give you trouble?"

"The territory's way big enough for everybody," Duncan said. "We'll likely not even see them again."

"I like your idea," Markham said. "But I don't think we'd ought to take Barrett and Coly too lightly."

"What do you mean?"

"I mean I think they'd try and get another gang together," Markham replied. "I think we'd ought to kill them. Then we'd be shed of them for good. There'd be no worry about trouble, or starting another gang."

"I can't argue with that," Duncan said. "But how do you figure we could pull that off?"

"Give me some time to figure on it," Markham said. "Just lay back and I'll set us a plan."

Duncan fell back to take his position driving the horses. He'd never dreamed on a reception like that. He had thought he'd have to talk to Markham several times before he agreed to go in with him.

Markham had actually been eager. Likely he had been thinking the same thing himself.

His idea of getting rid of Barrett and Sterns was a good one. Especially Coly Sterns.

Duncan smiled. Barrett would be gone. No more crazy orders. No more riding with troublesome women. Things would go a lot smoother.

He looked back to where Coly Sterns was riding by himself, whipping a willow against his leg. He would see to Sterns himself. It would feel good to get rid of him, once and for all.

Eighteen

INDHAM LED them along the Jayhawkers' trail, across the headwaters of the Medicine Lodge River, through the last segments of the cedar country.

He said little, his eyes peering into the distance. He wanted to catch the Jayhawkers before they reached their hideout along the Arkansas River. The Jayhawkers would likely want to change brands before moving the horses to one of the forts.

Windham knew that if they didn't catch the Jayhawkers before the hideout, the fight to get the horses back would be a whole lot tougher.

Near midday Windham noticed dust rising in a streaming cloud to the north and west. The others had seen the dust as well. Jenny was pointing, giving her idea of what was happening.

"I'd bet they're headed for the JY outfit," she said. "They raise horses to sell to emigrants and the army."

"Why didn't they head there first?" Stick asked. "Why would they ride out of their way like this and then turn west?"

"I said I'd bet that's where they're headed," Jenny said. "I didn't say I knew why."

"She knows the JY ranch," Jessie said. "Her husband used to work there. They were going—"

"Jessie, that's enough," Jenny said. "I don't need my life's history told right now. Besides, we haven't got time, not if we're going to head off those Jayhawkers."

"Do you know a way to cut them off?" Windham asked her.

"Yes, I know that country over there real well," Jenny said. "We'll be hard pressed to catch them before they reach the JY, though—unless we make very few stops."

Windham rode next to Jenny as she led the way across a sea of open grassland. She set their course at an angle to the rising dust, hoping to meet with it before the JY ranch.

They stayed in the saddle past sundown, through the darkness and into the dawn, stopping only to water the horses. Throughout the hard riding no one complained, not even Jessie, whose arm wound began to seep.

As the sun rose, Stick bandaged it with herbs, asking Jessie how he felt.

"Don't make no nevermind about me," Jessie said. "I can go as far as any of you, likely farther."

"You're looking a little pale," Stick remarked. "We'll stop if you want. Mr. Windham won't mind."

Jessie frowned. "I said I don't figure to hold anyone back. I can take it. Besides, I don't care what Mr. Windham thinks. He's turned out to be a liar."

"What do you mean?" Stick asked.

"It's between me and him," Jessie said.

Windham, who had overheard the remark, led his pinto over. "What have I lied to you about, Jessie?"

"You told me you'd teach me Indian ways," Jessie said. "Remember?"

"I remember," Windham said. "But when have we had the time?"

"Can't you teach me while we're riding?"

"I have to keep watch constantly while we're riding," Windham said. "You can understand that."

"If you'd teach me some Indian ways, I could help you watch," Jessie said. "Don't you figure?"

"That makes sense," Windham said. "We'll stop to rest around noon. You be ready then."

Jessie rode with new enthusiasm, shaking off his fatigue. The thought of learning even a little of what Frank Windham knew made him eager for the sun to rise high overhead.

At noon, they stopped in a spring-fed draw filled with cottonwoods. Though Windham was anxious to keep going, he realized that he had made Jessie a promise. Equally important was allowing the horses time to rest and graze.

After everyone had drunk their fill of water and had topped their canteens, Jessie asked if there was something to eat.

"You want to be alert for what I'm going to show you," Windham said. "If you eat, you'll dull your senses. You can eat tonight, when we bed down."

Jessie didn't complain. "I'm ready," he said. "Can we start now?"

"I'd like to learn, too," Jenny put in.

"Don't go horning in on this," Jessie said. "Mr. Windham said he'd help *me*."

"I'd think you would want your sister to learn this,

too," Stick spoke up. "There may come a time when she'll save your life."

Jessie thought a moment. He turned to Windham. "Do you reckon that's true?"

"It would be good for both of you to learn this," Windham said. "You'll be needing one another right along. It can't hurt."

Windham sat them both down on a log, facing a patch of gooseberry and wild rose. He told them to sit absolutely still and look into the brush.

After a time, Jessie asked, "What are we looking for—birds or something?"

"If you see birds, that's good," Windham said. "But I want you to look deeper. I want you to get to know that area in and around the bushes real well."

Jessie frowned. Jenny looked equally confused.

"It's important that you learn to see things," Windham said. "You have to learn that you don't just look at the world around you, but really *see* it."

Jessie looked at Windham. "All I see is just a bunch of leaves and branches and stuff."

Windham walked over and pulled two stems from a gooseberry plant. He handed one each to Jenny and to Jessie.

"Feel the leaves and the stem," Windham said. "Touch your fingers against the sharp prickles. Rub the tops of the leaves, and the berry that's almost ripe. Get a sense of what that plant is like. Remember it."

Stick was watching with interest. Windham had told him about his early days with the Cheyenne and how they had taught him to become one with his surroundings. It was a key to survival with them.

Stick likened it to his grandfather's teachings about working the fields and enjoying the feel of the cotton. "It don't matter that you're supposed to pick it for somebody else," his grandfather would say. "What's important is that you feel good about the touch, the softness, the fact that God gave you the fingers to touch it with."

At first Stick had disregarded his grandfather. He hadn't felt good about working for someone who had him in bondage. After a time, though, he had learned that his grandfather was right. When he finally let himself feel good about being outdoors and alive, the work became much easier.

In watching, Stick could see that Jenny and Jessie both had a good feel for the land. Windham was just teaching them how far they could go with it.

"Now sit and relax," Windham was saying. "Look at the leaves and the stems and the berries. Look at them closely. Remember how it felt to touch them with your fingers. In looking closely, you should get the same feelings going through you."

"Wow!" Jessie said. "It works. I can do it!"

"Yes, he's right," Jenny said. "It's amazing what happens. I can feel the leaves and stems as if I'm actually touching them."

"Now, the trick is to spend a lot of time at it," Windham said. "I was taught to sit for a full day, just looking at one place. I learned that I could feel every little thing about an area. If something seemed out-of-place, I could feel it without actually seeing it."

"Do you mean that if an enemy came, you could tell?" Jessie asked. "You knew there were enemies around without even seeing them?"

"That's right," Windham said. "When you learn to know an area and see everything that's there, anything different that comes into that area alarms you. You know that something or someone has come from outside the area. Warriors guarding a village have to know this. It works for hunting, as well."

"How long will it take me to be as good as you?" Jessie asked.

"That was rude," Jenny said. "You don't say something like that."

"I wasn't asking you," Jessie said. "I know I'm better'n you already."

"It takes practice," Windham said, "a lot of it. You don't ever totally learn it. You're always working at it."

"How could you sit all day, especially as a child?" Jenny asked. "I would have gotten bored."

"It's important to train yourself," Windham explained. "The younger, the better. To become good at anything takes a lot of dedication. A lot of it."

Windham got up and started for his horse. Jessie rose and caught up with him. "Would you let me ride in the lead for a while? I think I can see things better now."

"You'll get your chance to ride in the lead another time," Windham said. "We're after a bunch of killers. I don't want to take any chances."

"Do you think there'll be a time when I can use what I just learned?"

"You can use it right away," Windham said. "You can always practice watching all around you."

"Are there other things you'll teach me, Mr. Windham?"

"I can teach you some other things, when the time is right."

"Good," Jessie said. "That's real good. Those Jayhawkers had best not try and sneak up on us. They won't stand a chance."

Nineteen

THE DAY was passing quickly. Judd Barrett was nervous; they still hadn't reached the JY horse ranch. It was farther out than Del Brice had thought.

Time meant everything now to Barrett, who wanted to get the women and the horses back to the hideout. The change of the moon was nearing and he couldn't miss his appointment with the Jacobs bunch.

There were still a lot of unanswered questions: What about the renegade Cheyenne? Where were they? Were they still around to steal more horses and cause more trouble? He wondered if the army had taken care of them yet.

He knew that the army would be even more eager for horses if they were chasing renegade Cheyenne. For that reason, he was anxious to reach the JY and get their horses as well.

Another threat was Frank Windham and the others with him. Windham wasn't one to give up. He would still be coming. He would have to be dealt with.

Just ahead was a small stream, where they stopped to water the horses. Barrett's mind was on the Jacobs gang when Del Brice rode up to him, apologizing.

"I had forgotten how far out the JY is," he told Barrett. "But we're getting a lot closer now."

"You've cost us a lot of good time," Barrett said. "There'd better be a lot of good horses there."

"We'll get plenty of horses," Brice promised. "And we're close now."

"How can you tell?" Barrett asked.

Brice pointed into the distance. "This little stream tails off into a bigger one over that way. We can follow it down to a line cabin. A blind widow used to live there, where the trail crosses the creek. Maybe she's still there."

"A blind widow?"

"Yeah, the daughter of a trader that built the place. She's a breed woman. Part Kiowa. They say she knows medicine and such. She's a strange one, if she's still alive."

As a young man, Del Brice had seen duty at a Missouri military post, where he had become friends with a French trapper and scout. He had learned a bit about Indian religion and could understand some Sioux.

But he had always been afraid of Indians and their ways. He had seen the results of their torture techniques. When the renegade Cheyenne had come to the hideout for the horses, he had known better than to challenge them.

"That widow's lived there ever since her husband was killed by Comanches," Brice continued. "Folks say she's got powers."

"What kind of powers?"

"I can't say. I don't care to know. But she takes good

care of the cabin for the JY. They use it to gather range horses."

"You say it's a line cabin now?" Barrett asked.

"It's a big cabin," Brice replied, "built for a trading post, like it was. There's a good set of corrals there. Could be a lot of horses there now. But likely not. The roundup's been over for a while. From there it's a straight shot cross-country to the JY."

"You sure about that?"

"I promise, Judd. I know where I am, now."

"How far to the cabin?" Barrett asked.

"We should get there come nightfall."

"And then how far to the JY?"

Brice squinted. "Best I can figure, about a half day's hard ride."

"You ain't been figuring too well of late," Barrett reminded him. "You sure it's just a half day."

"I said a half day, hard riding."

"How hard? We ain't running these horses all over these plains!"

"Maybe just a little faster than we've been moving them," Brice said. "We're about there, Judd. Let's just do it."

"Of course I figure to do it!" Barrett said. "We've come too far, and we need more horses to sell. I'm just disappointed in your memory. You've made it real hard for us."

"I can't figure why you're so riled."

"Think about it, Brice," Barrett said. "First, you let the Cheyenne steal the horses we had back at the hideout. Now you lead us clear out here to hell, when you said you knew where we were going. You don't seem too worried that we've lost a full two days because of this."

"That ain't fair," Brice said. "I didn't invite those Cheyenne in. Besides, I told you they were around. And

I told you to wait on this raid until we had the horses rebranded and sold."

"I'm the one who says what goes, not you," Barrett said. "I figure you weren't watching so well when them Cheyenne came. You could've gotten the horses and everyone else out of there if you were."

"You ever fought Injuns, Barrett?"

"More than you have. A lot more."

"I doubt it. If you had, you'd ought to know that you don't always see or hear them before they get there." He glared at Barrett. "I don't figure you fought too many of them, otherwise you wouldn't be here now."

"You figure I can't hold my own, Brice?"

"Injun fighting's different."

Barrett stretched in his stirrups and rested his hand on his Colt. "Are you pushing me, Brice?"

"No, I wouldn't do that," Brice said. "I just don't see the reason you're so owly. I mean, what have we got to be in such a big hurry about?"

"We've got to get these women to the Jacobs bunch," Barrett said. "And the longer we keep these horses, the more trouble we're apt to have."

"Look, if it's Frank Windham you're worried about, we'll get him," Brice said. "We've got him outnumbered. When he comes, we'll get rid of him. And whoever else comes with him."

"I'm not worried about Windham," Barrett said. "I figure I know how to stop him. I just wished you knew your way out here, like you said you did. It's costing us time, and it's wearing these horses down. I don't like it!"

Brice frowned. "It's been a long time since I was across this way. It's a big country out here."

Barrett thought a moment. "Tell you what, Brice. I want you to send that young hand, Wilson, back up to the river. I want him to bring the Jacobs bunch down here. They know him. They'll come."

"I don't understand," Brice said. "Why do you want to bring the Jacobs bunch down here? This isn't their territory."

"I told them we'd meet them to trade by the change of the moon," Barrett explained. "Thanks to you, we won't get back there by then. We'll need the extra help. We've lost a lot of men to Frank Windham."

"Do you figure that's best?" Brice asked.

"Yeah, I do," Barrett said. "I'd send you with him, but I need you. Tell Wilson how to get back down to the crossing, where that widow lives. Get going!"

Brice rode off to find Wilson and get him on his way. Coly Sterns, who had been watering his horse, rode over to Barrett.

"Where'd Brice go?"

"You don't have to worry about it, Coly. Go over and tell Woods to untie them two women."

"What? You ain't really going to do that, are you, Judd?"

"You heard what I said, Coly." Barrett was breathing hard with anger. "Woods says they've been complaining that their hands are getting numb. I can't give them to the Jacobs bunch with bad hands. You do what you're told."

"I don't like it, Judd," Sterns said. "I don't like you giving them women a free hand. That ain't like you."

"You let me make the decisions," Barrett said. "For now, you just ride hard and do what you're told. If you do that, you won't have to worry about a thing."

"I'll do what you say," Coly told Barrett, "but I've got to tell you, I'm worried. I'm plumb worried about this whole thing."

Twenty

JUNE AND Karlie sat in the grass, rubbing their wrists. This was the first time their bonds had been loosed for longer than a few minutes since being taken by the Jayhawkers.

It had been Barrett's idea. June and Karlie had both seen him order it done.

Karlie realized that her complaints about numb hands had been taken seriously. It proved to Karlie that Judd Barrett was going out of his way now to insure their well-being. She didn't know why, but she knew that it was true.

All the Jayhawkers could see it as well. None of them could understand it, but it wasn't hard to see.

No one knew it better than a young Jayhawker named Billy Woods. He had been placed in charge of them. He had led their horses, tied in tandem, since the first night. He generally ignored them for the most part, having been told by Barrett not to harm them in any way.

He had untied them with indifference. He did what he was told. He might not always like it, but he obeyed. It was what he knew, all that he knew.

He had joined Barrett's bunch with a cousin, who had been killed by the sharpshooting woman when Coly Sterns had gone back after the four stray horses. He had felt dead for a while since then. Now he was beginning to grieve, in the only way he knew—with anger.

It bothered Woods that he had been forced to watch over the two women. Now, as the youngest of the gang, he had to do a lot of things the younger ones had been doing earlier—before they had been killed stealing horses from the trail herd.

A lot of the gang had been killed recently; more had died than at any other time before. This man they all talked about, this Frank Windham, he had to be real good with a gun.

Woods had been made to do a lot of the camp chores lately, but his biggest complaint was having to watch women he couldn't touch. It seemed odd to him that Judd Barrett had decided to keep these two fresh, just to please the leader of another gang. It didn't make sense.

After untying them, Woods stared a moment, then left to water his horse.

"I'll make sure he doesn't see another birthday," Karlie said.

"Don't go off half-cocked," June said. "I don't like him any better than you, but we can't just bust out against them. There's too many. We've got to plan things for when Jenny and that gunfighter catch up with us."

Since Karlie had "finally come to," as June kept putting it, she had generated a number of opinions about what had happened to them and what was going to happen to the Jayhawkers as a result. Her hatred for the

gang, especially Barrett and Markham, had been building steadily.

"I don't care about plans anymore," Karlie said. "I
want to get away from these men."

"Just a little more patience," June said. "Then we can
put this all behind us."

"No, I'll never feel right about myself again," Karlie
said. "They've ruined me."

"You shouldn't blame yourself, Karlie. Those men
gave you no choice. You were tied up, and they came at
you like a couple of animals."

"I mean to make it right," Karlie said. "I'll make
them pay for what they did."

"Just hold on," June said. "Jenny will catch up with
us soon. She'll give them what to."

"Jenny! Jenny! Jenny! Why wait for Jenny? I can do
a few things myself, you know."

June studied her daughter. Since her abuse, there had
begun a gradual and definite change in her personality.
Once shy and demure, she had turned into a bitter and
resentful woman.

June realized she shouldn't say a lot to Karlie. After
all, she had voiced and displayed her anger, especially
against the terrible little man they called Coly.

She had made life miserable for Coly. He was the
best one to pick on. None of the Jayhawkers liked him.
And Barrett kept him well in line.

"I think we should stay with Coly," June said. "He'll
go crazy and take it out on the others."

"Coly didn't . . . he wasn't part of that first night. It
was Barrett and that wrangler Markham."

"I know how you feel, but—"

"How could you know how I feel?" Karlie asked.
"Nothing like that has ever happened to you, has it?"

"Karlie, needn't be a stranger who forces you against your will."

"Are you saying Pa made you lie with him when you didn't want to?"

"I'm not saying anything, Karlie, except that a man in this country pretty much owns the woman he's married to. I don't need to say more."

"Well, these men don't own me, and they never will," Karlie said. "I won't let this go. I won't."

"What are you planning, Karlie?"

"I'll know when the time comes," Karlie replied.

"I'm telling you, we shouldn't push anyone but Coly," June warned. "The others have ways of getting back at us."

"I don't believe they could do anything to us now, not any more than Coly," Karlie argued. "Have you been watching Barrett? He keeps his eye on us real close. He wants us in good shape."

"The man is crazier than the others put together," June said.

"Not crazier than Coly."

"Oh, yes he is!" June insisted. "If he weren't, he wouldn't keep that little rat around. He's attached to him in some way, some sick way."

"I don't know about that," Karlie said, "but I know Barrett wants us safe and sound. What do you suppose he intends to do with us?"

"I've been thinking on that," June said. "I can't be sure, but I've overheard some of them talking about the Jacobs bunch and how they wished we were with them now."

"Do you figure Barrett plans to trade us, or something?"

"Who can say," June replied. "But we needn't worry. Jenny will make it here before long."

"She'd better," Karlie said. "I don't want any more men coming at me. I'll die before I let that happen again."

"Oh, Karlie, don't say that. I don't want you to die."

"I don't want to die, Ma. But if Jenny and that gunfighter don't show up real soon, I'm going to do something on my own. When that happens, someone's going to die. It might be me, it might not. But it's going to be somebody."

Twenty-one

ITH NO shade, the vast open was an oven, its floor a mottled brown and tan. The sea of dried grass, cured in the summer sun, rolled endlessly in every direction.

The Jayhawkers' dust rose in the distance, ever nearer. Windham had been judging the cloud, angling their course with Jenny's help to intercept it within a day.

Jenny had talked about an old widow, part Kiowa, who lived in a line cabin used by the JY horse ranch. Her cabin sat on the east bank of a small stream, beside a little-known crossing that led into the JY spread.

Jenny was concerned that the Jayhawkers would get to the widow first. "But I'm not really fearful," she told Windham as they studied the dust cloud. "The old lady can take care of herself. She can scare the wits out of you in a matter of minutes. She has powers."

"Do you mean she knows the spirit world?" Windham asked.

"Some people don't believe in such things," Jenny said. "I figure you do, though, since you lived with the Cheyenne."

"I know about it," Windham said. "She must be a special old woman."

Windham had known Cheyenne women who fit that description: very old and mystical, very close to the land and the mysteries of life. They said little, except when spoken to, and generally kept to themselves. Children sought them out for stories. Many traded presents and goods for herbal cures. They were treasured by the people.

"Why isn't she living with the Kiowa?" Stick asked.

"I don't know," Jenny replied. "She doesn't talk much and I never got to know her well enough to ask her."

"Jarrell must have told you, didn't he?" Jessie said. "Why don't you tell Stick and Mr. Windham about him? He was a good guy." Jessie lowered his eyes. "I still can't believe he's gone."

"We haven't got time to talk about any of that now," Jenny said. "We've got to reach the crossing."

As they rode, angling toward the dust in the distance, Windham thought about the Jayhawkers and how many lives they had ruined. Since beginning the chase, he had never allowed himself to think that they wouldn't catch them. He had always thought about what would happen when they did.

Jenny and Jessie had proved themselves strong and determined. Jessie's arm wound was still sore, yet he never said a word. They would know how to take care of themselves when the shooting started.

Windham's main concern was for June and Karlie. He

knew nothing about them or how they were being treated by the Jayhawkers.

He still couldn't understand why the Jayhawkers had taken them. He was beginning to believe, though, that the gang had needed someone to cook for them. And in Karlie's case, someone to use.

Windham believed that the two women would hold on, however, just like Jenny and Jessie. While saddling their horses that morning, Jenny had told Windham that her aunt and cousin could take a lot.

"June is a tough gal," Jenny had said. "She'll likely make it rough on one of them. She'll pick out the lowest and pick at him like an old hen. I'm not sure about Karlie, though. If they hurt her bad enough, she might just want to die."

"They would have likely killed her or left her, if that was the case," Windham said.

"Karlie has another side," Jenny said with a nod. "I saw it once or twice when we were school kids. She can be downright dangerous. I've seen her that way, and I wouldn't want her against me."

Everyone was anxious to keep riding, with no stops of any kind. But the horses would not keep up their pace unless allowed to rest and graze.

They stopped in an open slough at the head of a small drainage. A large spring seeped from the hillside and spread out into a boggy marsh.

Red-winged blackbirds rose from cattails, angered at the intrusion. Two blue herons lifted, flapping their giant wings, desperately trying to become airborne.

At the head of the spring, the water was fresh and pure. Everyone drank deeply and filled their canteens.

Deer and antelope trails coursed in from all directions. Jessie, who had been wanting to hunt for fresh meat, looked hard in every direction.

"Most of the deer and antelope are bedded down for the day," Windham told him. "They'll start coming out in the evening."

Refusing to give up, Jessie announced that he wanted to ride to the top of a nearby rise. When he reached the rise, he waved for everyone to join him.

"What do you suppose he found?" Jenny asked.

"I hope it isn't those renegade Cheyenne," Windham said. "Our horses are too tired for a chase."

At the top of the rise, Jessie was pointing into the distance. "What's standing out there?" he asked. "Is it a buffalo?"

"It looks to be an old bull, off by himself," Windham said. "We'll ride up to him real easy. He's apt to be in a foul mood."

Windham rode in front, taking note of the bull's actions. They rode slowly and stopped a short stone's throw away. The old bull pawed the ground and snorted, its tail curled over its back.

"We just wanted to say hello," Stick told the bull. "You could at least be a little friendlier."

Jessie's eyes were bulging. "He's huge! I don't think I'll try to shoot him. My bullet would just bounce off and make him even madder."

The bull was mottled white and dark brown, with a black mane of thick, coarse hair around the head and neck and along the shoulders and hump of the back.

"He's got white in his coat," Jessie said. "I've seen a few herds of buffalo, but never a white one."

"That makes him especially sacred," Windham said. "Even though this one's got a bad temper, he's very special."

"You know about that from the Cheyenne?" Jessie asked.

"Yes, I learned a lot about animals and how they

live," Windham said. "Animals are sacred, put here to help us in our daily lives. They provide us with food and clothing. Otherwise, we couldn't stay alive. There's a lot to be learned from them."

Jessie studied the bull. "What's going to happen to him?"

"He'll live by himself until he dies," Windham replied. "He's getting up in years, so that might be this winter."

"That doesn't seem fair," Jessie said.

"Everything has to die sometime," Jenny reassured him. "You know that."

"I suppose," Jessie agreed. "But something like a white buffalo should live forever."

"In a way, he will," Windham said. "You'll always remember seeing him. In your mind, he will never die. In the Indian way, you could consider him as a protector, if you'd like."

"How do you mean?"

"Just think of him as with you," Windham explained. "Feel his power with you, protecting you from harm. That way you can feel safe."

"That's good," Jessie said. "I'm glad to know that."

"In fact," Windham continued, "we've come upon clear water and a white bull, all in the same afternoon. That's a good sign. Our intentions are pure. We should meet with success."

"Does that mean that none of us will get hurt fighting the Jayhawkers?" Jessie asked.

"I can't say that for sure," Windham replied. "It means only that our journey is one that should have been made. We are doing the right thing. How our journey ends cannot be known yet."

The bull began to graze, moving slowly, swatting at

flies with its short, heavy tail. Jessie turned to Windham.

"I feel better about meeting the Jayhawkers. I was really worried for a while. I'm not as worried now."

"That's good," Windham said. "Let's go back to the spring and rest for a while. The horses need to graze and get strength for the last part of our ride. This will be the hardest and the most dangerous. We'll need to be alert. We'll have to be able to ride hard, for we won't get another chance."

Twenty-two

THE SUN fell toward the horizon, a round ball of red that shimmered in the late afternoon heat.

Judd Barrett reined in at the top of a hill and studied the large cabin below. The foundation was cottonwood logs, the rest made of sod. The building appeared in good shape, almost too good to be occupied by a blind old woman.

Nearby sat an elaborate set of corrals, just as Del Brice had described them.

With Barrett was Brice and Coly Sterns. The others drove the horses toward a creek which ran just beyond.

The widow sat outside the cabin, rocking slowly. Del Brice pointed down.

"That's the widow Rucheau. She's lived out here forever."

"You say she's blind?" Barrett asked.

"As any bat," Brice answered. "I don't know how she does it. Some say she's got special powers."

"Special powers?" Barrett said. "What are you talking about?"

"Like I said before, she's part Kiowa. She knows medicines and Indian things."

Barrett smiled crookedly. "Are you saying she casts spells and such?"

"I don't know," Brice replied. "I don't believe in such as that. It's hearsay."

"What do you figure she's got to eat down there?" Sterns asked.

Barrett spurred his horse. "Let's have a look."

The old woman wore a loose-fitting cotton dress with worn, high-topped moccasins. Her hair was white, done up in long braids that hung nearly to the ground. Her face, etched deeply by wind and time, was expressionless.

She didn't budge as Barrett and the other two dismounted. She rocked slowly, her chair squeaking loudly.

"Are you the widow Rucheau?" Barrett asked. He waved his hand in front of her face.

The woman frowned. "What's your business?"

"Oh, she speaks English," Barrett said. "I didn't think a breed could learn it."

"She like as not knows French and Kiowa to boot," Brice told him. "Breeds can speak everything."

"We heard you know this country," Barrett said. "We heard you've been here for a long spell."

"Pretty long," the widow said. "You've not been through. None of you."

"How would you know?" Coly asked. "You're blind."

"I know voices," the widow said. "And I can smell very well."

"We're passing through," Barrett said. "We need to rest up a spell. This is a good place to do it."

Sterns started for the cabin. "What you got inside, you blind old hag?" He laughed and entered. He quickly came out with a bundle of herbs that had been hanging from the ceiling, drying.

"Best leave them be," Brice cautioned.

"Why?" Coly asked. "They ain't no good for nothing." He threw them into the dirt and went back inside.

Barrett laughed. "You'll have to excuse him, widow. He's been on the trail quite a spell."

"What's wrong with him?" the widow asked.

Barrett disregarded the remark and pointed to a nearby garden. "Looks like you've got some potatoes and carrots there. You don't tend that yourself."

"Yes, I do."

Barrett studied her. "I don't believe you."

"You see others around here?" the widow asked.

Barrett looked back to the garden. "Them vegetables ready yet?"

"They could be."

"How about if you dig them?" Barrett said.

The widow shook her head.

Barrett spat tobacco. "That's not neighborly."

The widow rocked, remaining silent.

"We've got her now so that she won't talk," Brice said.

Barrett snorted. "That don't matter. Have Woods bring them two women over here to dig spuds and carrots. Tell the boys to corral the horses. We'll be eating good tonight."

"I'd watch them women close, if I were you," Brice said. "They're up to something."

Barrett waved him away. "Have Woods bring them over, like I said. I'll worry about them, not you."

Barrett was well aware that the two women were becoming a great problem, especially the older one. She was making it hard for Coly, who wasn't allowed to touch her. She kept taunting him, telling him that very soon he was going to "get his stupid butt shot off."

The woman wouldn't let go. She talked constantly about her sharpshooting niece and how close she was getting. The more she talked, the more confidence she gained.

Coly was going crazy. Between the woman and Ben Duncan, who laughed at Coly continually, Coly had no piece of mind. Something was bound to break soon.

Now the younger one had come back to life. After the first night, she had stared out into the distance for so long that it seemed she might never recover. That was over.

Now she looked around camp with angry eyes. She seemed to be scheming within her mind. It wouldn't be long before she caused major trouble.

The men wanted to have the younger woman again. But Barrett insisted they leave her alone. They became angrier each time he denied them.

His own desire was overcome by his belief that the Jacobs bunch wanted the women fresh. He had made a deal with them, and he stuck to his deals. He believed they would stick to their end, and his vision of a new and better gang would be realized.

For that reason, he guarded the two like a mother bear. He would continue to do so until Wilson brought Martin Jacobs and his bunch down to the crossing.

Jacobs and his men had better come soon. Barrett knew that he couldn't hold things together much longer.

Woods rode up with the women. They dismounted and Woods led their horses toward the corrals.

Karlie and June studied the widow. She appeared indifferent to the Jayhawkers, as if she didn't care what happened to her.

"Where's your digging tools?" Barrett asked her.

She rocked without answering.

"Did you hear me?"

Coly stepped out of the cabin, his mouth stuffed with fried bread. "There's some tools behind the door, here."

"Bring them out," Barrett said, "and take the women over to the garden. Make sure they dig a lot of spuds and carrots."

"Aw, Judd, you going to make me watch them?"

"Do it, Coly. They need to dig so we can eat."

Mumbling, Coly got the tools and herded June and Karlie toward the garden. Barrett looked past them, into the west, where the sun was nearing the horizon.

"Do you know anything about the JY horse ranch?" he asked the widow.

The widow rocked without speaking.

Barrett studied her. "Did you ever have anybody kick your chair over?"

The widow remained silent.

"You shouldn't be so high-minded," Barrett said. "Some day somebody will come along and kick that rocker of yours. Then you'll have to feel your way around to get up."

The old woman began to sing in Kiowa—high, wavering notes that hung in the air like sharp knives. Barrett watched her for a short time, then mounted and rode out toward the corrals.

Even when he got to the corrals, he could hear her. The men were unsaddling their horses and rubbing them down, all of them looking toward the widow.

"What's she doing?" Barrett asked Brice.

Brice was running a curry comb through his horse's mane. "I'd say it's some kind of spirit song. She's not happy, I do know that." He listened a while. "I can tell you that she's calling something. Maybe her spirit helpers. It gives me the creeps."

"You go over and tell her to stop," Barrett said.

"No, not me. I'm not going near her."

"I told you to make her quit."

Brice looked up. "I'm not going to, and that's it. I don't want to be near her anymore."

"Why didn't you tell me she was like that?"

"I didn't know you'd rile her so," Brice said. "I had no idea. All Injun women are like that."

Barrett shifted in his saddle. "I wished she'd quit that."

"I imagine she will directly," Brice said. "As soon as she's gotten what she wants."

"And what would that be?" Barrett asked.

"Revenge," Brice replied. "Likely revenge of some kind."

Barrett dismounted and unsaddled his horse, the widow's singing echoing through his head. He wanted to scream at her, but knew it would do no good.

Now more than ever he wished he hadn't decided to head for the JY horse ranch. It had been a bad decision. A very bad decision.

Twenty-three

JUNE AND Karlie were digging, filling sacks with potatoes, carrots, and onions. They had been quiet, listening to the widow's high songs.

The widow stopped singing and Coly Sterns walked over. He stood above them, smiling, slapping his willow against his leg.

"I'm glad she quit that howling. It's a good thing that we don't have her with us, too."

"You don't like us with you?" June asked.

"That ain't funny," Coly said. "But it won't be long now until we're shed of you two. The Jacobs bunch can use you up."

"The Jacobs bunch?" Karlie said. "Who are they?"

Coly smiled. He reached down and pulled a blade of grass, broke it off, and began picking at his teeth.

"You just don't worry. They'll take good care of

you." He walked to the edge of the garden and yelled out to Barrett that he was tired of being in the garden.

Karlie whispered to June, her voice filled with anger. "I'm not waiting any longer. I've decided to get a gun and kill as many of these men as I can."

"Now hold off, Karlie," June said. "We'd best wait for Jenny and that gunfighter to catch up with us."

"I'm tired of waiting," Karlie said. "Besides, who's to say they'll even get here?"

"You know Jenny. She won't give up. She'll stay looking for us until she finds us."

"Well, she may not have enough time to catch us," Karlie argued. "If they plan to trade us to another bunch of Jayhawkers, we're as good as dead. I won't go through it again. I'm going to get us out of this."

"What do you aim to do, Karlie?"

"I'm thinking on it. Maybe I can work on Woods."

"How?"

"I'll figure a way."

"You women hurry up!" Sterns was walking back toward them "You're taking way too long. You've got cooking to do."

"We're hurrying," June said.

Coly turned to watch Barrett and the others as they came from the corrals. Karlie let out a little shriek and jerked back from a potato plant.

Coly turned around. "You let a toad scare you?"

"I don't like toads," Karlie said.

"Watch out or he'll *eat* you." Coly laughed, then turned around and began whipping the willow against his leg.

Karlie pointed down under the potato plant. June could hear the buzzing.

"A rattler," Karlie whispered. "It's not very big."

"Take that hoe and kill it," June said.

"No, I'll just trap it."

"For heaven's sake, Karlie. Why wouldn't you kill it?"

Karlie trapped the small rattler with the hoe, pressing behind its head. She reached down and took it just behind the jaws, pinching it between her thumb and forefinger. She slipped it into a small sack of onions.

"Karlie, what are you doing?" June asked.

Karlie motioned. "Come over here, Coly, and help me dig a couple of onions."

"What are you going to do?" June hissed.

"You just watch," Karlie said.

"No, Karlie, it's not a good idea."

Coly was walking toward them. "What did you say?"

"I said I wish you'd dig an onion and stick it in this bag for me," Karlie said. "I'd be much obliged."

Coly stood a ways distant, whipping his leg with his willow. "I don't aim to help you dig. Just bring what you've got."

Barrett yelled from the cabin, "Coly! Get them women and vegetables up here. What's holding you up?"

"Coly, you want to help me, don't you?" Karlie said. "I know you do. Hurry!"

Coly stared. "You've gone crazy. You just bring what you've got. Now!"

Again Barrett yelled from the cabin. "Coly! What the hell you doing down there?"

"We're coming, Judd," Coly yelled back. "We're coming."

Karlie got up, holding the small onion sack in one hand and a sack filled with potatoes in the other.

"You leave that snake here, Karlie," June said.

"I know what I'm doing," Karlie whispered, starting out of the garden. "You don't say anything."

June picked up sacks of potatoes and carrots. "Karlie, don't do it."

"Listen to you," Karlie said. "The whole time we've been captive, you've spouted off. Now you want to quit on me."

"Karlie," June said, "leave it to Jenny and that gunfighter. Let them do it."

"We can't wait for Jenny and that gunfighter," Karlie said. "It's time we did something for ourselves."

At the cabin, Karlie left the small sack in the shadows along the outside wall. The sun had fallen completely and Barrett was making sure all his men were back from the corrals.

At the same time, he was arguing with Ben Duncan. "I know what I'm doing, and I want the Jacobs bunch to come down and help us," he was saying. "I make the decisions here."

"There's no reason for that," Duncan argued. "We don't want them taking a cut."

"We're short of men," Barrett said. "We need them."

June and Karlie passed the widow. The widow's head rose slightly and turned to one side.

"Can you hear the snake?" June asked her.

The widow nodded.

"Will you help me talk sense into this girl?"

"Is she doing something wrong?" the widow asked.

"Yes, and she'll get us all killed. She will."

"Just drop it!" Barrett yelled to Ben Duncan. "The Jacobs bunch is coming down and that's that." He turned to June. "What are you doing there with that widow? Get inside and start cooking."

June started for the door. She took a quick look back. The widow was smiling.

Twenty-four

KARLIE LUGGED two sacks of potatoes into the cabin. June followed with the carrots. One of the men had placed a washtub full of water on the table.

The cabin was roomy, with two support beams in the center. A wood stove and table rested near one end. There were no other furnishings, except a buffalo robe rolled up in one corner and a grass-tick mattress covered by a deerskin.

The walls were lined with drying herbs. Jayhawkers began coming in, carrying saddles and other tack for repair. Some began knocking the herbs down for fun. Others settled into cleaning weapons or working on their riding gear.

Barrett lugged his saddle through the door and picked a prime spot near a large lantern. June and Karlie dropped the vegetable sacks near the table. June tossed carrots and potatoes into the water and began scrubbing them while Karlie turned for the door.

"We've got all the vegetables," June hissed. "Where are you going?"

"I'm not after vegetables," Karlie replied.

June stared hard. "You leave that snake out there."

"It belongs in here," Karlie said, "with the others."

Ben Duncan walked in, carrying a rifle. He sat down and began cleaning it, and resumed his argument with Barrett.

"I wish you'd listen to me for once," Duncan said. "We don't need to throw in with the Jacobs bunch. We can bring those horses from the JY back here and change the brands on all of them, then take them right to the fort. We don't need help. We've got enough men."

"I already made the decision," Barrett said. "I figured we needed more men, and the Jacobs bunch do things like we do. They hate Rebels more than we do."

"That's really all this is," Duncan said. "You're fighting Rebels, not doing a business in horses."

Dirk Markham, who was shuffling a deck of cards, spoke up. "I see it the same as Ben. We don't need the Jacobs bunch moving in on us."

"I don't care how you see this, Markham!" Barrett yelled. "I'll do the deal making round here. If you don't like it, you can hit the road. Jacobs has a better wrangler than you'll ever be."

Markham glared at Barrett. "You plan on replacing me, do you?"

"If you don't like my orders, then you'll go," Barrett said.

Karlie had eased through the men and had left the cabin. She now stood over the small sack. The widow was rocking in the twilight.

She slowed her rocking. "Your name is Karlie. Am I right?"

"How could you tell it was me?"

"I've learned to know people by other things than sight. You lift the sack very gentle. No problems."

Karlie took the sack and started for the door. The sack was moving. She dropped it. The buzzing began again.

"Be not in such a hurry," the widow said. "Gently. Very gently."

Karlie lifted the sack again, slowly, and opened the door. Inside, Barrett continued to argue with Duncan and Markham.

"I've had my fill of you two deciding what's best for this outfit. That's going to stop. Now!"

Markham shuffled his cards. "Maybe you'd better look around, Barrett. Do you think any of us wants the Jacobs bunch horning in? Think about it."

Some of the other men agreed with Duncan and Markham, while Coly and a few others sided with Barrett. Coly started yelling, switching his willow against the wall.

There was so much noise in the cabin that no one noticed Karlie come in with the small sack. No one noticed her holding it out from her side, and no one heard the buzzing.

She placed the sack on the dirt floor next to the table and the buzzing stopped.

"He's right," Duncan told Barrett. "We all put a lot of time into getting these horses. And we went along with you on riding way out here to the JY. We'd ought to have some say."

Karlie began washing potatoes. June cut a carrot into chunks and leaned over. "You've gone crazy. You know that, Karlie? It used to be your cousin Jenny who pulled the fool stunts. Now you've become just like her."

"It's about time," Karlie said. "I should have become like her well before now."

Barrett took time out from his argument with Duncan and Markham. "You women get a move on with them spuds and carrots. We ain't got all night."

"We need some help here," Karlie said. "There's too much work for just us. We can't get it done before late tonight. And that's the truth."

"Coly, you go over there and give them a hand," Barrett said. He told Woods to go with him.

"Aw, c'mon, Judd," Sterns said. "I don't want nothing to do with those women."

"They won't bite you," Barrett said. "Now go on over there and help."

Sterns continued to complain. Woods, disgruntled as well, stood with his arms crossed and his head bowed. Duncan and Markham began to laugh.

Karlie elbowed June and smiled. "Maybe I can get Coly to fetch me an onion after all."

"Leave it be, Karlie," June warned. "He's got that big knife, you know."

"He'll want an onion, Ma."

"He's not right in the head, Karlie. You don't know what he'll do. If he gets bit, he'll go crazy."

"I'd like to see it," Karlie said. "I can't imagine him being any crazier than he is now. But if that's possible, I'd like to see it."

Twenty-five

COLY CONTINUED to argue with Barrett against working with June and Karlie, stomping on the floor, whipping his leg with the willow.

"It ain't fair, Judd! You make me do women's work. How about the others?"

Barrett studied a slight tear in the latigo strap of his saddle. He could reinforce it with rawhide.

"Judd, I said I don't like this. Why are you making me do it?"

"I want you to make friends with those women," Barrett replied. "I don't want no hard feelings between you."

"What?"

"That's right. I don't want you to think about whupping them all the time. Maybe if you work with them, you'll find out that you like them."

The men were laughing. Coly couldn't understand

why Barrett would make him out a fool. Something was going on inside his cousin's head. Coly knew it. Something was wrong.

"Then these others should have to make friends with them, too," Coly said. He pointed to Duncan and Markham. "Why shouldn't one of them have to cook? Why me?"

"Because I told you to," Barrett said. "Now, you're wasting time."

"I'll tell you what, Coly," Markham spoke up. "How about if I deal three cards? I'll give you one, Duncan one, and then one to myself. Lowest card has to help cook. What do you say?"

Coly readily agreed. He had nothing to lose. He calmed down and sat on the floor, while Markham shuffled.

"You, Woods," Barrett said, "I want you to go over with those women and get to work. You don't have to wait."

The other men began talking again, working on their tack or cleaning their guns. Woods unfolded his arms and walked over to the table.

He wedged himself in between June and Karlie, and took a potato from the washtub.

"Make sure they're clean before you go to peeling them," June said.

Woods frowned. "You don't go telling me what to do."

"She's just trying to help you," Karlie said. "You see, if one of those spuds has dirt on it and one of your friends sees it, they might not be happy. In fact, they might kill you."

Woods laughed. "Who you trying to kid? Most of these men wouldn't even notice. So don't either one of you get an idea to start riding me. I won't take it."

"That's good," Karlie said. "I can see that you've got what it takes. Do you plan to lead this bunch someday?"

"Who can say. I know that I don't want any guff from a couple of women." He began cutting the potato he had peeled, dropping pieces into an empty bucket.

"I was hoping that Barrett would have you come over and help," Karlie said. "I've been wanting to talk with you for a while. I just haven't gotten the chance."

"What kind of game are you playing?" Woods asked.

"I just think that you're going to be a leader someday, that's all," Karlie said. "You're Billy. Right?"

"Yeah, Billy Woods," he replied. "Maybe, when you're with the Jacobs bunch, you'll hear of me from time to time."

"Why would we want to be with the Jacobs bunch?" Karlie asked. "We're perfectly content to stay with you and the others."

"Perfectly content, eh? You haven't been acting perfectly content."

"Well, maybe I could be more content. Maybe if I got to know you a little better, I could be real content."

"That don't add up at all," Woods said. "You fight like crazy against Markham and Barrett the first night. Then you don't say anything for a long time. You just stare into space. Now you're saying you'd like to know us better."

"I said I wanted to get to know *you* better," Karlie corrected him. "I didn't mean anyone else. In fact, that's what bothered me so much. I don't care at all for Markham or Barrett. And I heard that Markham told Barrett not to let you see me, that it wouldn't be good. Is that so?"

"Barrett don't want anyone near you," Woods said. "He wants you and your mother fresh for the Jacobs bunch. He says Jacobs' men plan to swap some good horses for you."

"How do you feel about that?" Karlie asked.

"It makes no nevermind to me."

Karlie reached down and began to rub his leg. "I would miss having you around. I mean it."

June backed up and leveled a kick into Karlie's lower leg. Karlie turned to her and frowned.

"What's the matter with her?" Woods asked.

"She's always been that way," Karlie said. "She don't want me with nobody, especially someone I take to real strongly."

"Do you mean it?" Woods asked.

"I've been watching you," Karlie said. "You should have been able to tell, for heaven's sake."

Woods laughed sheepishly. "Come to think of it, I guess I do remember you looking at me."

"You bet I have," Karlie said. "I've just been trying to figure out a way to tell you. This is the only way I could."

Behind them, Markham had finished toying with the deck. Coly was suspicious, so Markham let him shuffle and handle the cards as much as he wanted. He took them back and began to deal.

He gave Coly the first card: a ten of hearts. Coly whooped, certain that someone would draw lower. Duncan then got a queen of diamonds. Coly frowned.

Markham quickly dealt himself a king of spades. "Sorry, Coly. You lose."

Coly was cursing. "That ain't fair. Why didn't you let me deal the cards?"

"You agreed to this," Markham said. "You should have spoke up earlier if you didn't think it was fair. Now it's done."

"Judd, I ain't going over there with those women."

Barrett looked up from his work. "Yeah, you are, Coly. Get a move on. Now!"

Coly stormed over to the table. June moved out of the way as Coly reached a dirty hand into the washtub and pulled out two carrots. He took his big knife and began cutting them into chunks, dropping them onto the table.

"You going to make friends, Coly?" Woods asked. "These women are right friendly."

"You trying to make a joke, Woods?"

"No, I'm serious."

"You just tend to your own work," Sterns said. "You just leave me be. All of you."

Karlie tilted her head and looked at the small sack. "Coly, could you help me a minute?"

"I said I didn't want nothing to do with any of you."

"I just want you to pick up these onions," Karlie said. "You can have the best one all to yourself."

"What onions? Who said I liked onions?"

"I don't know why you wouldn't," Karlie said. "Are you telling me that you don't like onions?"

"Maybe from someone else," Coly answered. "But I don't like any onions you'd have. Now, leave me be."

"Well, I guess I'll just have to get the onions for you," Karlie said. "One way or the other, you're going to help me with the onions."

"Karlie, he don't like onions," June said. "You heard him. Leave him alone about the onions."

"You take her advice," Coly said. "You leave me be."

Billy Woods spoke up. "I'll get them for you. Would you like that?"

Karlie paused, then answered, "Sure, if you want. I guess that would be real nice. Be sure and offer Coly the first one, though."

Twenty-six

IT WAS well after dark when they stopped to eat. Stick passed out handfuls of pemmican. Jessie sat cross-legged, his head slumped down.

"Jessie, wake up and eat something," Stick said. "You can't sleep just yet."

Jessie jerked his body erect. "I'm not sleeping. No, I'm not."

"We'll sleep for a while," Windham said. "But we've got to get going again soon."

"We should make that crossing by sunup," Jenny said. "It won't take hard riding, either."

Jenny's voice was low and filled with weariness. Windham knew it was going to be hard to awaken them once they got to sleep.

Jenny finished her pemmican and stood up. "I don't think we should stop at all. I think we should keep riding."

"What about Jessie?" Stick asked.

"He can ride double with me," Jenny said. "He'll ride in back and lean on me to sleep. I'll tie him to me so he won't fall off."

"That will put a big strain on you," Windham said.

"I'll make it."

"I can ride by myself," Jessie said.

"No, I want you to ride double with me," Jenny insisted. "If we're going to catch them, we have to keep going."

"Then we'll take turns," Jessie said. "I'll sleep for a while, then change with you. That's only fair."

"Jessie, you can't hold me up on a horse," Jenny said.

"Yes, I can," Jessie insisted. "That's the way it's going to be."

"We'll see," Jenny said.

"No, we won't see," Jessie told her. "We'll take turns, or I don't ride double with you."

"Let's not waste time arguing," Windham said. "Let's get started. You can work the details out later."

They mounted and started again, onward as the sun fell and the night settled in, the air hot as the breath from a stove. A pale moon shone down on a flat and treeless land, open in every direction. Had the land been rough, it would have been difficult to stay on their horses. Even Windham felt drained to the bone.

Jessie, tied to Jenny, fell sound asleep during the first mile. The jostling never disturbed him, his head bouncing against his sister's shoulder.

Jenny never complained, though the strain was evident when they stopped briefly to water the horses.

Windham and Stick had eased Jessie off onto the

ground, where he lay fast asleep. Jenny had to be helped down, as her legs were cramped.

"Just give me a minute," Jenny said. "I'll be fine. Just give me a minute." She began to drift off to sleep.

"How far do we have to go yet?" Windham asked her. "Jenny, how far away is the crossing?"

Jenny rubbed her eyes. "We'll make it. We'll get there before sunup."

"Jenny, how far is it from here?" Windham asked.

"I'd say around three hours," Jenny replied.

"Are you certain?"

"I know where we're at, Frank," Jenny said, an edge to her voice. "I might be half-dead, but I know where we're at."

"I just wanted to be sure."

"We've got a good six hours until daylight," Stick said. "If we could get close to the crossing, we could take some time to rest."

"That's a good idea," Windham said. He looked at Jenny, who had slumped over.

"Maybe it's the Lord's will that we don't catch those Jayhawkers," Stick said.

"That's a fine attitude," Windham said. "I thought you wanted your other horse back."

"What I want and the Lord's will aren't always the same," Stick pointed out.

"In this case, the two are the same," Windham said. "We've just got to push ourselves."

"I don't think that's a problem for you and me," Stick said. He pointed to Jenny and Jessie. "But look at these two."

"I've got an idea," Windham said. He pulled the broken locket from his pocket and placed it in Jenny's hand. "This is Karlie's," he said, waking her up.

Jenny lifted her head. "What did you say about Karlie."

"Look in your hand," Windham said.

Jenny held the locket up. Stick struck a match.

"Where did you get this?" Jenny asked.

"Back at the first campsite," Windham said. "I found it while reading sign."

"Why didn't you tell me?"

"You were upset enough as it was. I didn't think you needed to see it just then."

"Damn you!" Jenny said. "You had no right to keep this from me!"

Jessie rolled over on the ground and sat up. "What's all the shouting?"

"Don't worry none," Stick told him. "Your sister and Mr. Windham are talking."

"I figure there's more to it than that," Jessie said.

"I'm asking you why you kept this from me," Jenny said to Windham.

"I thought it was in your best interest at the time," Windham replied.

"Just how do you have the right to judge my best interests?" Jenny asked. "You God or something?"

"I'm sorry, Jenny," Windham said. "Maybe I should have given it to you then. But you've got it now."

"You bet I've got it now," she said, rising to her feet. "And I'm going to see that Karlie gets it back." She started for her horse.

Jessie looked from Jenny back to Windham and Stick. "She's got a determination, I'd say. I'd best catch her."

Stick and Windham started for their horses. "You got her riled but good," Stick said. "That was sure enough a slick trick."

"I didn't see any other way," Windham said. "We need to make that crossing, or we'll likely lose our chances at those Jayhawkers. I figure we've got a chance now. The Lord's will, I guess."

"No doubt about that," Stick said, climbing into the saddle. "Certainly no doubt about that."

Twenty-seven

WOODS, YOU stand back. I'll get the onions."
Ben Duncan had walked over and was
standing behind Karlie.

"I can get them," Woods said.

"Just back away," Duncan told him. He stepped in
front of Woods and smiled at Karlie. "I should think
anyone would want to help a pretty lady. But then, Coly,
he's too dumb to know any better."

Coly glared at Duncan. "I'll gut you one day. I promise."

"Keep on dreaming, Coly," Duncan said. "One of
these days you're liable to wake up dead."

Duncan knelt on one knee and began to open the
sack. He looked up at Karlie, telling her how much he
liked onions, slipping his hand in.

The buzzing started. Duncan jerked his hand from the
sack. "Damn! There's a rattler in there!" He checked the

back of his hand, where two tiny red holes had appeared just behind the knuckles of his first two fingers.

Karlie screamed and jumped back. She grabbed June and said, "Oh, how awful!"

Duncan pulled his pistol and began shooting into the bag. Pieces of snake and onion and burlap flew everywhere.

Barrett and the others hurried over.

"A damned rattler bit me!" Duncan explained.

Coly was standing back, his eyes huge. Then he started laughing.

Duncan turned his pistol on Sterns and fired. The hammer clicked on an empty chamber. Coly blinked. Barrett jerked the pistol from him.

"What's going on here?"

"I got snakebit and he thinks it's funny," Duncan said. "I got bit! I need a doctor!"

Coly turned to Karlie. "You wanted *me* to get them onions, didn't you? It's your fault. You put that rattler in there!" He lifted his knife from the table.

June stepped in front of Karlie. "Don't you try nothing crazy, you stupid bastard!"

Coly lunged at June, but Barrett grabbed him and twisted his wrist until the knife fell, then threw him over the table, knocking the tub sideways. It slid off the edge, dumping water and vegetables everywhere.

Coly came off the table. Barrett grabbed him by the back of his shirt, at the neck, and jerked him around.

"Damn you, Coly! I said never to do that! What's the matter with you?"

Coly was choking. Barrett loosened his grip.

"Them women put that rattler in that bag," Coly said, holding his throat. "They're trying to kill us all!"

"We did no such thing!" June yelled. "I would never

have gone into that garden had I known there were snakes in it."

"How'd the snake get into the bag?" Barrett asked.

"How should I know?" June replied.

"Look," Karlie said, pointing to where the wall met the ground, "there could have been one come under that log. See, there's a hole. I saw a mouse go out of there earlier."

"Not likely," Coly said. "You was playing with something in the garden."

"A toad," Karlie told him. "You said so yourself."

"I *asked* you if it was a toad," Coly argued. "I didn't *see* no toad."

"It was a toad," Karlie said. "I don't play with snakes."

"Then who done it?" Coly asked. "How did that rattler get in here?"

"Maybe the widow done it," one of the others said. "Maybe she called it in with all that singing she did. Maybe she did it."

"I'll bet she loosed it in here on us," another said.

"She's blind!" Markham yelled. "She couldn't do something like that."

"That don't keep her from singing them songs of hers, though," Woods said. "We all heard her, making them sounds and all."

"Maybe she put more than one in here," Karlie suggested.

The room grew quiet. Everyone began to look around and check their gear.

Duncan was leaning against the wall, sucking on the back of his hand, his face ashen. Barrett was watching him, wondering if Duncan had any sores in his mouth.

Barrett had known a man whose brother had been bitten. The man, with sores in his mouth, had sucked on the wound. Within an hour his head had swelled up like a pumpkin.

But Barrett wouldn't tell Duncan that. Let him find out for himself.

"I need a doctor," Duncan told Barrett. "You've got to get me to a doctor."

"I don't have to get you anywhere," Barrett said. "You can get yourself to a doctor if you want, but I'm not taking you."

"I can't go alone," Duncan argued.

"Find someone to take you, then." He looked around the room.

Markham came forward and tied a rawhide tourniquet around Duncan's wrist. "That ought to keep the poison from moving."

"Will you get me to a doc?" Duncan asked.

Before Markham could answer, Barrett spoke up. "Maybe we can find you a doc after all. I've just decided that we're all leaving here tonight."

"We've leaving tonight?" Markham said.

The men began to mumble. "But we ain't eaten yet," Coly complained. He picked up one of the potatoes from the floor and bit into it.

Barrett ignored him. "I don't think any of you want to stay in this cabin," he said, "not after what's happened. I'll take whoever wants to stick with me and ride north with the horses. We'll meet the Jacobs bunch. They shouldn't be far from the crossing. Those of you who side with Markham can go with him and take the JY horses. You can have them."

"Are you talking about breaking the bunch up?" Markham said.

"That's it," Barrett replied. "No sense in sticking together if we don't see eye to eye."

"I can't go with Markham," Duncan said. "There's likely no doc at the JY."

"Ride with me, then," Barrett said. "After you see a doc, you can join Markham. I don't care what you do. Go on out and saddle up."

Duncan pointed to his hand. "I can't saddle a horse."

Barrett squared his jaw. "You need a doctor, don't you?"

"Yeah, I do."

"Then saddle your horse. No one's going to do it for you. You'd best get going."

Brice had been in a corner, talking with Woods about the situation. Both agreed they didn't like some of Barrett's ideas, but they couldn't see joining with Markham.

"Woods and me, we've decided to stay with you," Brice said. "Do you figure we'll meet up with Jacobs and his bunch?"

"They should be pretty close," Barrett said. "We'll meet up with them and they can help us change the brands. Then we'll take the herd to Fort Dodge."

Brice took a lantern and left. Woods and Duncan followed. Markham stood in the corner with three men who wanted to join with him.

Coly continued to eat vegetables from the floor. "What we going to do, Judd?" he asked. "I can't figure this."

"Just do what you're told, Coly," Barrett said. "Get out to the corrals and saddle your horse. And saddle two for these women."

Coly picked up his willow and slapped himself continually as he left.

Barrett stepped outside and began pacing. Markham and his new followers went by him, hurrying toward the corrals.

Barrett stopped Markham. "I want to talk to you."

"Why are you doing this?" Markham asked. "I don't get it."

"I told you," Barrett said, "I can't have men following me who won't do as I say."

"But giving us the JY horses? You've come a long way across here. I don't know why you'd give them up just like that."

"You've got to take them, don't you?" Barrett pointed out. "That might be easy, it might be hard. I figure it's a fair trade, your share of these horses for whatever you can get from the JY."

"Yeah, I suppose," Markham said. "You going to find a doctor for Duncan?"

"I'll do what I can."

"Sure," Markham said. "Just give him a decent burial."

Barrett watched Markham hurry to the corrals. He laughed to himself. A decent burial for Duncan. You bet.

Markham didn't know he was headed for his own grave. He could go to the trouble of stealing the horses from the JY, but he wouldn't have them for long.

Barrett had it all figured out. When Jacobs and his bunch showed up, they would all ride toward the JY. Markham and those with him would be giving up the horses, and be lowered into a hole, all at the same time.

It would all work nicely. Just so the Jacobs bunch arrived before daybreak.

Twenty-eight

INSIDE THE cabin, June was hissing at Karlie. "Look what you've gone and done. Why couldn't you listen to me?"

"I don't care which one of them got bit," Karlie said. "Why should you?"

"That's not the point. We would have been better off to keep picking on Coly. That way he could have caused trouble for Duncan and the others. Coly would have taken his anger out on them. Then they could have shot one another up and we could've just watched."

"But they're split up now. That will make it easier for us."

"I don't know how," June said. "Barrett wants to leave here now, just because you got one of them snake-bit. We'd have been better off to wait it out."

"Maybe *you'd* have been better off," Karlie argued,

"but that doesn't mean I would have. It was just a matter of time until one of them came at me again."

"What are you talking about, Karlie? You tried to get Woods all worked up."

"I figure I can get him alone and get his gun. Can't you see what I was working toward?"

"You're taking an awful lot of chances."

"I told you I was going to do something. We've been with these men too long. I can't stand it any longer."

"One more day," June said. "If you could've stuck it out just one more day."

"Then what?" Karlie demanded. "What would have happened in one more day? Jenny would have come to our rescue? Jenny and that gunfighter? How do you know for sure?"

"We might not ever know for sure now," June said. "We might not live through this. If Barrett takes us out of here tonight, and they meet up with the Jacobs bunch, it will be too late for help from Jenny and that gunfighter. And the way you've been blaming this all on the widow, he's liable to shoot her."

"Barrett won't do anything to her," Karlie said. "He's afraid of her. They already think she's a witch or something."

"But it's not fair to blame her," June argued.

The sound of Barrett's voice came from just outside the door. He was yelling out to the corrals for everyone to hurry. He entered the room and took a lantern from the table. He fixed his eyes on Karlie.

"I want some straight answers. What do you know about that snake?"

Karlie began to act horrified. "I've never seen nothing like it," she said. "I know there wasn't a snake in that onion sack when I brought it in. I just know there wasn't. I'd bet the widow did it somehow."

"Coly says you took it from the garden," Barrett said. "He says you found it there."

Karlie shook her head. "You saying I just picked it up and put it in the sack? Does that sound right to you?"

"Coly says he's sure of it."

"Then why didn't Coly say something about it before?" Karlie asked. "Do you think he'd stand here and cut potatoes if he thought there was a rattler at his feet. I don't think so."

Barrett thought a moment. "Maybe you're right. So what happened in the garden?"

"There was a toad in the garden," Karlie said. "Coly knows that. He asked me why I was afraid of it. Ask him about it."

"He said something about a toad," Barrett acknowledged, "but he said he didn't see it. He just *thought* it was a toad. I want to know about the rattler. I don't want any of my new bunch to get snakebit."

"We have no control over that," June said. "Don't be ridiculous."

"I still figure you two had something to do with the snake," Barrett said. "I'm telling you. Jacobs bunch or not, if another of my men gets bit, I'm going to kill you. Both of you."

"Then you'd better kill the widow, too," Karlie said. "She's been singing a lot of songs. You know, maybe she was singing to the snakes."

"That's crazy," Barrett said. "Plumb crazy."

"Well, you heard her," Karlie said. "Just before Duncan got bit, she was singing. She's been singing the whole time."

Barrett went to the doorway and stared out at the widow, who sat in the darkness, her rocker turned out toward the open prairie. He pulled his pistol.

"Yes," Karlie said. "Hurry and shoot her. You know

what they say: women like her are worse on you after they're dead."

Barrett turned. "What are you talking about?"

"Look around this cabin," Karlie said. "You and your men have torn down her medicine herbs. You've angered her protective spirits. If you kill her, they'll all come after you."

"What kind of foolishness is that?" Barrett said.

"Shoot her and see if it's foolishness," Karlie taunted.

Barrett holstered his gun. He tied June and Karlie tightly, his face drawn with anger.

"I don't want any more trouble from you two," he said. "I've had enough."

"Why don't you just let us go, then?" Karlie asked.

"I don't aim to do that," Barrett said.

"Then you can figure on more trouble," Karlie told him. "I know some of the same kinds of tricks that the widow does. Maybe there'll be more rattlers."

Barrett raised his hand to strike her. His eyes were large and filled with anger. Karlie stood firm.

"Go ahead," she told him. "Hit me as many times as you want. But I'll bet the Jacobs bunch won't like it."

Barrett lowered his hand. "What do you know about the Jacobs bunch?"

"Coly told us all about it," Karlie said. "That Coly, he's got a big mouth. He told us everything."

"What did he tell you?" Barrett demanded.

"I won't say." Karlie was smiling. "You'll have to ask him what he told us. It was plenty."

The sounds of horses outside the cabin brought Barrett to the door. Woods and Duncan rode up. Duncan was slumped over his horse.

Barrett herded June and Karlie outside. Duncan was complaining about dizziness. He leaned over his horse and vomited.

"He needs a doc bad," Woods said.

Barrett ignored him. "Where's Brice and Coly?"

"Coly's still saddling the horses for the women," Woods replied. "Brice wanted to stay at the corrals until Markham and the others left. He was worried they'd steal the horses, I guess."

The sounds of horses splashing through the crossing carried through the night. Markham and the others had left.

"Go back to the corrals and tell Coly to come up here," Barrett said. "He should have those horses saddled by now."

"Coly might not come back from the corrals," Karlie suggested. "Maybe he got snakebit, too."

"I told you to quit making trouble," Barrett said. He was wondering if keeping these two for the Jacobs bunch was even going to be worth it. But he had no choice. He had made a deal and felt he couldn't back out.

"If the widow put a snake in the cabin, then she could have put one in the corrals, too," Karlie reasoned. "That's all I'm saying."

"I'm sick," Duncan said. "Get me to a doc." He fell off his horse and lay moaning, half-conscious.

Woods sat his horse, staring down at Duncan.

"Woods, you go to the corrals and get Coly, like I said!" Barrett yelled. "I'll take care of Duncan."

"What are you going to do for him?"

"Don't worry about it. Get to the corrals. Now!"

Woods rode off. Barrett dragged Duncan to the cabin and sat him up near the doorway. He lifted a lantern.

"Duncan, can you hear me?"

Duncan's hand had nearly doubled in size. His lower lip and the entire right side of his face appeared ready to burst.

"Duncan, you're going to die. Did you know that?"

"No ... don't want to die," Duncan said. "Get me ... to a doc."

Behind, the widow began to sing again in Kiowa. Barrett lurched to his feet. He grabbed June by the arm.

"Tell that widow woman to quit that wailing," he demanded.

June pulled away from him. "I can't make her quit. You go talk to her."

Coly and Woods rode up. Coly was leading one horse.

"Where's the other horse?" Barrett asked. "These women can't ride double. We've got to move fast."

"That mare the younger one's been riding's gone lame," Coly said, dismounting. "I didn't know which one you wanted me to use instead."

"Coly, can't you make a decision for yourself?" Barrett asked.

"I'm sorry, Judd. I just wanted to be sure, that's all." He looked to Duncan. "Is he about dead?"

"He's sick," Barrett replied, "but he might be a long ways from dead yet."

"He treated me poorly, Judd," Coly said, smiling, whipping his willow against his leg. "I know what to do with him."

Barrett smiled slightly. He felt a strange lust growing within him.

Coly was holding his knife handle, easing the blade up and down in its sheath. "Can I, Judd? Let me, Judd. Let me."

Barrett forced June over to the horse and pushed her into the saddle. He made certain she was tied tightly and put Karlie on behind her. He turned to Woods.

"Where's Brice?"

"He's waiting at the corrals. He's ready to go any time."

"Good," Barrett said. "Take these two women to the corrals and saddle a horse for the younger one. I don't care which horse, just a gentler one. We don't want her getting bucked off. Coly and I will be down directly. We'll leave from there."

"Why don't we all go together?" Woods asked.

"Go on down, like I say," Barrett insisted. "Coly and I'll follow directly."

Woods took a lantern from Barrett. He rode toward the corrals, leading June and Karlie behind him on the horse.

Barrett turned to Coly. "Hurry and get it done. We've got to ride out of here."

Coly had his knife out, testing the blade against his thumb, smiling at Duncan. "I figured it would be harder than this," he was saying. "What with you just laying up against that cabin, it won't be much of a fight. But it'll be good just the same. It'll be real good."

Twenty-nine

WINDHAM LOOKED across the prairie through the darkness. A sea of shadowed grass lay still under a very pale moon. The night sky showed Windham that midnight was approaching. It worried him, for they had become lost.

Jenny, who was sitting her horse next to him, said, "I feel so foolish, but I think we rode too far south. I know now that the widow's cabin is along that creek we crossed a ways back. I should have been watching better."

"It's an honest mistake," Windham said. "We're all pretty tired."

"I don't want the blame for missing those Jayhawkers," Jenny told him. "I could never forgive myself."

"Don't be thinking that way," Stick said. "Where's the JY horse ranch from here?"

Jenny pointed. "I figure it's due west. I'd say we've come in a straight line with the crossing. If we turn back east, we should run right into the cabin."

"We should be in pretty good shape, then," Windham announced. "Since the dust stopped rising in late afternoon, the Jayhawkers should still be at the cabin."

"They probably used the corrals to hold the horses overnight," Jenny said. "We shouldn't have any problem catching them before sunup."

Stick rocked in his saddle. "I've been waiting for this since we started. I guess the time's about come."

Windham dismounted. "We'll let the horses graze a while. They'll need the strength once we hit those Jayhawkers."

Everyone hobbled their horses and loosened the cinches on their saddles. There was plenty of grass, so the horses would get their fill quickly.

Jessie started for a small rise. "I'll keep watch," he said. "I want to use my Indian training."

"You won't go to sleep, will you?" Stick asked.

"Not a chance. I'm learning how to watch all around me. I want to see how it works at night."

"Don't go too far," Jenny said. "Stay where we can see you."

Jessie waved. He walked a ways distant until the shadows swallowed him.

Everyone sat down to rest. Jenny looked through the darkness toward the rise.

"Jessie's braver than I am," she said. "I think I would have been afraid to wander off in the dark at that age."

"It doesn't seem to bother him," Windham noted. "He's a strong kid."

"I worry about him, though," Jenny said. "He's growing up too fast."

"Can't be helped sometimes," Stick put in. "It's the Lord's will."

"I don't want to talk about the Lord's will right now," Jenny said. "So far, the Lord's will hasn't been in my favor."

"You can't take offense at the Lord," Stick said. "He has His ways."

"Well, I can't understand His ways," Jenny said. "My husband was as good a man as there was, yet he died awfully young. He and I were very happy together. We didn't get much time to enjoy it. I don't see the fairness in that."

"Nobody said we understood His ways," Stick argued. "Sometimes they don't seem fair at all. We can't do nothing but try and learn from life."

"I don't know what I'm supposed to learn," Jenny said. "I'm too confused."

Stick nodded. "Yeah, I know that one. I've been confused since the day I was born. I don't figure it will get any better, either."

Windham was watching the rise where Jessie had gone. He saw a figure running through the grass toward them.

Jessie was out of breath when he reached them. "Riders!" he hissed, pointing behind him. "A number of them coming toward us. They could be Jayhawkers!"

Windham was on his feet. "Did you see loose horses with them?"

"No," Jessie replied. "I just saw the riders. I didn't wait. I figured you'd ought to know."

"I'm glad you came right away," Windham said. He started for the horses, the others following.

Stick slapped Jessie on the back. "That was smart thinking. I'd hire you as a scout any day."

Windham was taking the hobbles off his pinto. "Get your horses ready to ride," he told the others. "But stay here and wait for me to come back. I'll see who they are."

"Can I come with you?" Jessie asked.

"Stay here and keep your rifle ready," Windham insisted.

"But I saw them first," Jessie argued. "I should get to go out with you."

"It's good that you were watching," Windham told him, mounting. "It's likely that you saved us some bad trouble. But you can help me more by waiting here with your sister and Stick."

Jessie nodded reluctantly. He dismounted and stood with Jenny and Stick, watching Windham ride into the darkness, knowing he couldn't fight like Windham and would only be in the way.

Windham rode his pinto around the edge of the rise, careful not to silhouette himself against the sky. In the distance, he counted four riders coming straight toward him.

They weren't driving horses ahead of them, making Windham wonder if they were Jayhawkers. On the other hand, who would be riding across the plains at midnight?

Windham thought about it. It could possibly be someone who had also lost horses to the Jayhawkers and was trailing them. There was no easy way to tell.

Windham dismounted and lowered his pinto down into the grass. He tied the reins to a large leadplant and folded a foreleg back, whispering a Cheyenne word into the horse's ear, a sign to lie still and quiet.

Windham studied the riders as best he could through the darkness. A warm wind began to blow, hot and oppressive, coming suddenly from the southwest.

A strange feeling came over Windham. The Cheyenne used to say that a hot wind brought bad luck to someone. Windham was certain bad luck was coming. He just hoped it was for the Jayhawkers.

Thirty

T AKING ADVANTAGE of the breeze, Windham moved to where the horses wouldn't smell him. He took position in the grass, lowering himself so that he was nearly flat on the ground.

The riders approached, talking among themselves. As they drew nearer, Windham heard the name Barrett.

"Barrett has to be crazy," the lead rider was saying. "He wouldn't just set us loose on our own, to take the JY horses for ourselves."

Another rider said, "I've been thinking about that. Maybe he figures we'll get the horses, then he and the Jacobs bunch will take them away from us."

"I've wondered about that myself," the lead rider said. "That's why we're pushing so hard. We'll get there and take the horses, then go clear to Fort Hays with them. Barrett and Jacobs will pay hell catching us."

Windham now realized he had been chasing Judd

Barrett, older brother of Kelly Barrett. That explained the false grave that had been laid out the first night.

Barrett wanted revenge for the death of his younger brother. But it also sounded like the Jayhawkers were having serious internal problems, big enough problems to have broken them up.

And who was the Jacobs bunch? It bothered Windham. They didn't need another bunch of Jayhawkers joining Barrett. The odds were already heavy against them.

Windham crouched, motionless. The Jayhawkers were nearly upon him, still discussing how they would steal the JY horses and make their escape from Barrett and the Jacobs bunch.

As he watched, Windham realized that the third rider was mounted on Stick's missing horse, Jackson. He had planned on letting them pass and joining with the others to head for the crossing. He quickly changed his mind.

Stick had come a long ways to find his horse, a horse that meant a great deal to him. Windham wasn't going to let the opportunity to get Jackson back escape him, no matter what the odds were.

Windham remained crouched. The lead rider passed, followed by the second. When the third rider was nearly next to him, Windham sprang.

Windham grabbed the roan's bridle as it jumped sideways, throwing its rider. He steadied the horse and clubbed the Jayhawker over the head with his Colt.

The other horses had also shied. One of the Jayhawkers had fallen into the grass and another had caught his boot in the stirrup. His horse bolted and he screamed as he was dragged through the grass.

Dirk Markham struggled to stay in the saddle. At first he thought a bear or a cougar had attacked them. Now he knew it was a man.

Markham believed it was a renegade Cheyenne. He wasn't going to wait for more to show up and spurred his horse into a dead run back toward the crossing.

From somewhere behind Windham, a lick of flame spat into the night. Dirk Markham fell from his horse and lay still.

Windham settled Stick's roan and patted its neck. He looked out into the darkness. Jenny had to be out there somewhere, waiting to fire at another Jayhawker.

The Jayhawker Windham had clubbed with his pistol was groaning, holding his head. The one who had been thrown was now on his feet. He began to fire wildly.

The big roan began to skitter. Windham worked to hold him, while more shots came from the darkness behind. The Jayhawker turned, yelling, staggered a few steps, and fell.

Windham settled the roan down. When the horse had relaxed, it began to graze peacefully. He walked over and untied his pinto.

Windham felt the breeze against his face. Stick and Jessie emerged from the darkness.

"You were gone way too long," Stick said. "We figured you needed some help."

"Where's Jenny?" Windham asked.

"Here," Jenny called. She emerged, holding Dirk Markham's gunbelt.

"That was quite a shot," Windham announced.

"I've done my share of night hunting," Jenny said. "I always give them a running start."

Windham approached the Jayhawker he had clubbed. "Can you hear me?" he asked, taking the Jayhawker's gun and sticking it in his belt.

The Jayhawker groaned. "You broke my skull."

"You'd better worry about your neck now," Windham said.

"How'd you know who they were?" Stick asked.

"I crept up close enough to hear them talking," Windham replied. "The leader's name is Barrett. I killed his younger brother a couple of years ago in a shoot-out."

"So that's what the grave was all about," Stick said. "The leader was going to make you a dead man."

"That's it," Windham said. He pointed to the roan, grazing nearby. "There was one other reason I knew who they were. Do you recognize that horse?"

Stick eased over to the roan. "Jackson? You got Jackson back!"

"It's him," Windham said. "Safe and sound."

Stick took the reins. "Jackson! Good Lord in heaven, it is you!" He began hugging the roan, planting kisses on its nose.

Jenny walked over to the injured Jayhawker, who was rubbing his head. She stuck the barrel of her rifle in his ear.

"This is just to say hello."

"Don't shoot," Windham said. "Maybe we can get some information from him."

"We don't need nothing from him," Jenny said. "I'd just as soon do him in."

"He's already down, Jenny," Jessie said from behind. "Save your bullets."

Jenny lowered her rifle. "Who are you people?" the Jayhawker asked.

"My name is Frank Windham. I don't know your name, but I do know that you and the others are a murdering bunch of Jayhawkers."

"Not me," the Jayhawker said. "I don't know what you're talking about."

"You didn't raid a cattle herd along the Cimarron, and steal the remuda?"

"No."

Windham pointed to Stick's horse. "Then where did this roan come from?"

"We found him wandering around out here. You must be looking for another bunch."

"Are you telling me that two of you were riding double until you found the roan?" Windham asked. "Not likely."

"Let's hang him," Jenny said. "Let's ride until we reach the creek, and then let's find a strong tree and hang him."

"Do you just hang people without a cause?" the Jayhawker asked.

"We've got cause," Jenny said. "Besides stealing our horses, you gutted my uncle and you took my aunt and her daughter. You know what I'm talking about. June and Karlie. Ever hear of them?"

"No," the Jayhawker replied. "Never heard of them. And I never heard of anyone named Barrett."

"Who said anything to you about Barrett?" Windham asked. He pointed to Stick. "I was talking to this man. What do you know about Barrett?"

The Jayhawker held his head, saying nothing.

"You were speaking about Judd Barrett, weren't you?" Windham pressed. "And what about this Jacobs bunch?"

The Jayhawker remained silent.

Windham looked to the others. "Barrett must be at the crossing, where the widow lives. As near as I can figure, Barrett is supposed to hook up with another bunch of Jayhawkers."

"I'd say we should head over to the crossing, then," Stick said. "Maybe the rest of our horses are over there."

"What are we going to do with him?" Jenny asked, pointing to the Jayhawker.

"We'll take him with us," Windham said. "He can tell us what he knows."

"Then we'll hang him," Jenny said. "Or maybe we should gut him, like he did my uncle."

"That wasn't me," the Jayhawker said quickly. "That was Coly Sterns, a dirty little man, kin of Barrett's. I don't even own a knife. I didn't even want to ride with them."

"You made a poor choice, then," Stick told him.

"They made me ride with them," the Jayhawker said. "I had no choice."

"Do we want to hear his sad story?" Stick asked Windham.

"No," Windham said flatly, "we don't."

Windham caught one of the loose horses and, after tying the wounded Jayhawker's hands, pushed him into the saddle. He tied him securely to the pommel and mounted his pinto.

"How did you learn to fight like an Indian?" the Jayhawker asked Windham.

"I used to live with the Cheyenne," Windham replied. "Compared to them, I don't know how to fight."

"I wouldn't bet against you," the Jayhawker said. "I've never seen anyone come up out of the grass like that. I'd rather be on your side."

"You should have thought about that when you joined up with Barrett," Windham pointed out.

"The point is," the Jayhawker said, "I hate Barrett. If you'll let me live, I'll fight with you against Barrett. I can help you."

"In your condition, you can't help anyone," Jenny said.

"Maybe you're right." The Jayhawker suddenly kicked the horse into a dead run.

Jenny jumped from her pony and took careful aim,

leading the Jayhawker slightly. Her rifle cracked. The Jayhawker flipped backward into the grass, the horse continuing on.

"Guess he thought he'd lose us in the dark," Stick said.

"He didn't know that Jenny's got eyes like an owl," Jessie declared.

"And a very sharp aim," Windham added. "Very sharp."

"Thank you," Jenny said. "But you should have let me finish him to begin with. We just wasted precious time on him."

"I gave him the benefit of the doubt. And didn't you say that you always allow a running start?"

"Yeah, and I gave him a running start," Jenny replied. "He couldn't have asked for more than that."

"It won't be that easy with the rest of them," Windham said. "Let's just hope they're all as foolish."

Thirty-one

A HOT wind had come up. In her rocker, the widow had begun to sing once again.

Tied tightly, June and Karlie sat quitely on the horse. Woods led them, looking back often toward the cabin. The corrals, filled with milling horses, lay just ahead.

"Does Barrett let Coly butcher everybody he wants?" Karlie asked Woods.

"I try to stay out of it," Woods replied. "I just do what I'm told."

"What happens when it's your turn?"

"It won't be my turn." He swung in the saddle toward the cabin, frowning at the widow's singing. "I wished she'd quit that!"

"What's going to happen when Coly wants to take his knife to you?" Karlie repeated. "Do you actually think Barrett's going to stop him?"

"I said that won't happen," Woods insisted.

"How can you be so sure?" Karlie asked. "It's bound to happen. If Barrett gets so he doesn't like you, Coly will pull his knife."

"Quit trying to rile me up," Woods said.

"You don't want to be a part of this," Karlie told Woods. "Why don't you ride away with us. You know I like you."

"I don't know any such thing," Woods said. "You touched my leg in that cabin, but you're not after me. You're trouble."

"Wouldn't you rather worry about me than Coly and Barrett?" Karlie asked. "I'm telling you, someday Coly will use that knife on you. You know he will."

Woods said nothing. He dismounted and hung the lantern on a nail near the gate. Through the night, over the wind, came the widow's singing.

Woods tied June and Karlie's horse to a corral pole and left them sitting on the animal. Brice sat in the saddle, staring back at the cabin. "I hate that singing," he said.

"Go stop her, then," Woods told him.

"Where's Barrett?" Brice asked Woods. "Where's Coly and Duncan? Why didn't they come with you?"

"Duncan's real sick," Woods replied.

"I know that," Brice said. "So why aren't they here? We need to ride and find a doc."

Woods was in the corral, selecting another horse for Karlie, checking its feet to be certain it wasn't lame.

"I think Coly plans to gut Duncan," he said. "In fact, I'm certain of it."

"What? That's crazy!"

"I figure everything's gone to hell," Woods said. "I just do what I'm told."

"Why didn't you stop them?"

Woods was leading the horse to the gate. "I don't want them gutting me, too. Coly gets a taste of blood and he don't want to quit. Barrett's worse, watching him do it, and all."

From the cabin there came a high-pitched scream. It grew louder, and more shrill.

June began to weep. Karlie clenched her teeth, knowing that her father had undergone the same torture.

"For God's sake!" she said. "You men stand by and let a thing like that happen?"

Brice spurred his horse. "She's right. Who knows where this will end. I'm going to stop it!"

"You're a mite too late," Woods called after him. "Don't you think?"

Brice didn't hear him. He was riding hard through the darkness.

Woods came out of the corral with another horse. He threw a blanket and a saddle over its back.

Karlie whispered into her mother's ear. "I'm going to jump off and untie the reins."

"No," June said. "You can't get it done before he catches you."

"I can try."

Woods was straightening the saddle. He started to whistle.

"I'm going to do it now," Karlie said, "while he's thinking about something else."

Karlie was getting ready to jump down when, from the darkness north of the cabin, five riders appeared.

Woods stared. June and Karlie both tightened in fear.

"Oh, God, no," June said under her breath. "That must be the Jacobs bunch."

"This should be interesting now," Woods said, tightening the cinch.

The riders drew nearer to the cabin. Karlie took a deep breath to clear her head.

"So, Mr. Woods, it looks like you're going to finally be getting rid of us."

"Not a moment too soon," Woods said.

"You know, Woods," Karlie continued, "I know now why you haven't touched me. You aren't a man, are you. You aren't able to be a man. It has nothing to do with Barrett telling you to leave us alone. No, you aren't a man."

Woods looked up at her. "You'd better be careful."

"You've been in charge of us all along, yet you can't even enjoy me. Barrett and Markham got their way the first night and you watched, just wishing you could do it."

Woods clenched his teeth. "I told you to watch your mouth. I mean it. Watch your mouth!"

"Men like you are worthless, Woods. You're no different than a little boy, a tiny little boy who doesn't know what life is all about. You need your ma to hold on to, don't you."

Woods came over and pulled Karlie off the horse. She fell to the ground, kicking and yelling.

"I'll show you what I can do." Woods struck her along the side of the head with the back of his hand. He grabbed at her blouse and began to tear it away.

June jumped down from the horse and kicked Woods from behind. The blow came up between his legs, dropping him like a stone.

Up near the cabin, the riders were slowing their horses. In the background, the widow was singing.

While Woods lay groaning, Karlie and June backed up to one another and worked to loosen their bonds.

When Karlie was free, she pulled Woods' pistol from its holster.

Woods was on his knees, straining to rise.

Karlie raised the pistol, cocked it, and pointed it at Woods' head. "Say your prayers. You're going to die."

Thirty-two

BRICE HAD returned to the cabin. He had hoped to stop Coly from butchering Duncan. But Woods had been right; he was too late. Duncan's middle had already been ripped open.

Duncan lay in a daze, watching his intestines ooze out onto the ground. Behind, in her rocker, the widow continued to sing.

Coly was smiling, licking the blood from his knife. Barrett's eyes were fixed on Duncan's stomach.

"You are really crazy!" Brice yelled to Barrett. "You let that sick cousin of yours kill one of our own men?"

"You stay out of it," Barrett warned. "Duncan had already turned against us. We'd have had to kill him anyway."

"What about Markham? You didn't kill him."

"That's coming," Barrett said. He pointed to where riders were approaching. "Jacobs and his bunch. They made it. We're joining with them. We'll take the JY horses from Markham and then he and the others will say good-bye, just like Duncan."

"Why didn't you tell me this before?" Brice asked.

"I wanted to see whose side you were on," Barrett answered. "I'm glad you picked me. Are you glad?"

"Yeah, I'm glad, Judd," Brice said. "Real glad."

Martin Jacobs rode up with his men and sat his horse. He was a tall, lean man with a patchy gray beard and hard blue eyes. He wore a wide-brimmed brown hat and a brown suit, coated in trail dust.

Riding with him were five trail-worn men, each of them with his hand on his gun.

"You can settle down, boys," Jacobs told them. "We're among friends."

"Where's Wilson?" Brice asked Jacobs. "Didn't he lead you down here?"

"He's about three miles back," Jacobs said. "We didn't need him anymore."

"So he left you?" Brice said.

"Something like that," Jacobs replied, grinning. He turned his attention to Duncan, lying near death in a widening pool of blood, and looked at Barrett. "You start getting rid of your men already?"

"Never too early to start," Barrett said.

"Looks like you're butchering a beef to me." Jacobs was eyeing Coly. "You plan to eat him?"

"Maybe," Coly said. "I ain't decided for certain yet."

Jacobs looked to Brice. "How about you? Want him to cut you a steak?"

Brice frowned. "I don't cater to that kind of thing."

Jacobs turned back to Barrett and pointed to Brice. "He one of them?"

Barrett nodded. Jacobs pulled a pistol and shot Brice

three times in the chest. Brice stared, his mouth open, and toppled from his horse.

"Why'd you have him do that, Judd?" Coly asked.

"Had to, Coly. We're starting fresh."

"You mean just you and me, and this bunch?"

"Never you worry about it," Jacobs said, reloading his pistol. "You and your cousin Judd, here, are in with us from here on out."

"Is that right?" Coly asked.

"That's right," Barrett replied. "We'll have a good bunch that will stop every grayback Rebel that tries to enter this territory."

"What about Woods?" Coly asked.

"He's got to go, too," Barrett said.

"But he ain't really done nothing."

"That's the problem," Barrett said. "He never gets anything done. He's watched the women, but he can't do much else."

"You going down to the corral and do it?" Coly asked.

"It'll happen when the time's right, Coly," Barrett said. "You just lay back."

"I'll rest easy," Coly said. "I just wish you'd have told me."

Jacobs smiled at Coly. "It's a right nice surprise, wouldn't you say?"

Barrett looked to Jacobs. "There's four more of them headed a piece west to steal some horses. We'll find them and take the horses away from them tomorrow, if that suits you."

"Suits me," Jacobs said. "I figure our deal will work out good." He looked toward the widow in her rocker, who had started singing again. "What's that wailing all about?"

"She's been up to that since we got here," Barrett replied. "She's part Injun."

"I'd like for her to quit," Jacobs said. "Me and my men could use some sleep." He looked around. "Where's the two women I've been hearing about?"

Barrett pointed toward the corrals. "Down there. We had aimed to ride up north a ways and join you." He pointed to Duncan. "This man got snakebit here. I don't like staying where someone's been snakebit."

"Don't bother me," Jacobs said. He looked around to his men. "Any of you worried?"

All of Jacobs' men agreed there would be no problem staying in the cabin for the night.

"Why don't you have those women brought up here so we can start bedding down?" Jacobs suggested.

"Where's the horses you said you'd swap?" Barrett asked.

"I didn't figure it was smart to drive them down here, and then drive them back," Jacobs said. "They're up on the river. Some of my men are watching them."

"Maybe that's not good," Barrett told him. "We lost some horses and two of my men to renegade Cheyenne."

"Your horses are safe," Jacobs insisted. "I've got four men watching them. They're safe. Now I'm interested in the women."

Barrett turned to Coly. "You go and bring them up here. I don't care if the horses are saddled. It don't matter now."

"I'll go fetch them, Judd," Coly said, sheathing his bloody knife. "I'd be plumb happy to."

Thirty-three

KARLIE HAD the pistol nearly in Woods' face. June hurried to her side.

"Don't shoot him. The others will hear it. They'll come down here to check."

"No. He's going to die. Right now."

"Think about it, Karlie," June said. "Don't shoot him. Let's just get on the horses and ride. Save the bullets for later, if we need them."

"Maybe you're right," Karlie said.

She started to lower the pistol. Woods charged her, knocking the pistol free, ramming her fiercely.

Karlie fell back against the gate. Woods gripped her throat with both hands. From behind, June kicked him again. He grunted and turned, swinging at June. Karlie pulled the lantern off the nail in the gate pole.

Woods turned as Karlie slammed the lantern into his

head. Shattered glass flew everywhere. Woods staggered sideways, coated with kerosine and flames.

Screaming, Woods ran, his shirt and pants ablaze. He fell into the grass at the edge of the corrals, rolling like a log on fire.

Flames licked along the nearest corral, spreading through the tall grass. The horses inside squealed, wide-eyed, breaking over the poles, running out into the night.

June and Karlie tried to mount, but the horses pulled free.

"Horse or not, I'm making a run for it," Karlie said.

"We've got to free the rest of the horses first. They'll burn to death."

"Let's do it." Karlie picked up Woods' pistol from the dust. "But we'd better hurry, or the fire will have us as well."

Coly was staring, his mouth open. He had just gotten started for the corrals when he had heard Woods screaming. Now he could see Woods ablaze, rolling through the grass, leaving a trail of flames.

Coly rode back to where Barrett and Jacobs had come around the cabin. Everyone was staring out at the burning corrals.

"What the hell!" Barrett was yelling. "What's going on down there?"

"I just saw Woods running," Coly said. "He was all afire. I don't know what happened."

Flames were spreading everywhere. Some of the horses were still trapped.

Coly pointed. "Look! One of them women is opening a gate. She's letting the horses out."

Barrett cursed. "Let's round them up. We can't lose them."

Jacobs was ordering his men to spread out and circle the running horses.

"I could help with the women," Coly said, gripping his knife. "We can't let them get away." He licked his lips, tasting remnants of blood.

"You put that knife away," Barrett told him. "Go get them women. Keep them in the cabin till we get all the horses back. But don't go harming them."

"What if the cabin gets afire?" Coly asked.

"Then get out of it," Barrett said. "Do what you have to, Coly. Just don't let them get away. And make sure they're in good shape."

Coly was licking his lips, a faraway look in his eyes.

"That's right," Jacobs said. "We want them just the way we bargained for them."

"Good," Coly said. "That's real good."

Barrett rode out with the Jacobs bunch to catch horses. Coly rode toward the corrals.

"They're mine now," he said, laughing to himself. "Judd said not to use the knife. I won't right away." He pulled his pistol. "I'll wing them first. Then, when they're down, I'll finish them how I want."

Karlie carried Woods' pistol into the shadows. She and June lowered themselves into the grass. They had seen Coly riding toward them.

They watched as Coly got off his horse and dropped the reins. The frightened horse rushed off into the night. Coly didn't seem to mind, so intent was he on finding where they were hiding.

He walked toward them, holding his pistol in one hand and his willow switch in the other, whacking himself along the leg.

"Come out, now, you ladies," he was saying. "I'm fixing to be nice to you."

"Karlie, what are we going to do?" June hissed. "He's almost here!"

Karlie was working with the pistol. "I'd shoot him, but the hammer's stuck halfway back. I can't get it to move."

Coly stopped barely twenty feet from where June and Karlie huddled in the tall grass. Everywhere around was chaos. Barrett and the Jacobs bunch were yelling, trying to catch the horses, while the flames crackled in the grass, spreading everywhere.

In the distance, behind the cabin, the widow's singing continued.

"You women come out now, you hear?" Coly said. "I want you to come out and talk to me."

Karlie struggled with the pistol, fighting to get the hammer to spring loose.

Coly walked closer, peering into the grass. "I know you're here. I saw you go down. You'd better get up."

The flames were moving all around. If the wind changed, they would be burned almost immediately.

Coly was starting to get nervous. He switched harder with the willow. "I want you to come out," he said. "Come out! Come out! Come out!"

Karlie continued to struggle with the pistol. She thought about throwing it at him, but she worried about missing.

Coly Sterns had lost patience. "This is your last chance," he said. "Stand up, or I'm going to start shooting into the grass."

Sterns didn't wait. He began firing, spraying a pattern of bullets near June and Karlie. They zipped through the grass, narrowly missing the women.

He laughed. "I'll flush you out, won't I!"

"We've got to do something!" June hissed. "We can't

stay here. We have to stand up and surrender, or he'll kill us!"

"Don't you understand?" Karlie said, pounding the pistol against the ground. "We can't stand up. He'll kill us for sure then."

"You do what you want, Karlie," June said. "But I'm not going to be shot here like a dog."

June started to move. Karlie held her down. Coly was getting closer, shooting all around them. He stopped to reload, just as Karlie got the hammer to come loose.

"I've got him now," Karlie said. "I'll end this right now."

Karlie rose and leveled the pistol at Coly. He stood with his mouth open. The pistol misfired. Karlie pulled back the hammer. It stuck again.

Coly recovered his senses and pulled his knife. He didn't want to take the time to finish reloading his pistol. He started for Karlie, his face contorted in rage.

June was up and running. Karlie aimed the pistol, cocked the hammer, and fired.

The bullet slammed into Coly's shoulder, spinning him around. He lost his balance and tumbled into the grass, screaming as he hit the ground.

Karlie tried to cock the pistol. Again, it jammed. Coly rose to his feet, wearing a strange grin on his face. His knife had entered his lower abdomen on the right side.

"Come here," he said to Karlie. "I'm going to show you how this feels."

Thirty-four

THE NIGHT was heavy, the moon losing itself behind a thick bank of clouds. From the west, on the wind, a storm had come. Thunder rolled and streaks of lightning flashed.

In the distance, a light formed and began to grow.

"That looks to me like fire," Stick said.

"We've reached the crossing," Jenny announced. "The cabin! They must be burning the cabin!"

"It's time we were there," Windham said, nudging his pinto into a run.

As they neared the crossing, Windham drew his pistol. Stick held his Colt Dragoon high. Jenny and Jessie both rode with their rifles ready.

The night seemed to be on fire. The corrals were ablaze, the grasslands filled with flames, lighting up the sky for miles around.

Through the light, Windham could see horses crossing the creek, scattering in all directions, followed by riders who swung quirts and lariats.

Upon seeing Windham and the others, the horses changed course, charging off to the side and back through the ranks of pursuing Jayhawkers.

The startled Jayhawkers quickly discovered Windham and the others bearing down upon them. They pulled their guns and opened fire.

Flame shot through the darkness. Bullets whizzed past Windham's head.

"Jessie, head for the cover of the trees!" Windham yelled.

"The hell I will, Mr. Windham, sir! I'm going to help out!"

"This is what we came for!" Jenny added.

"The good Lord be with us!" Stick said.

Overhead, the sky boomed and the lightning grew ever closer. Jayhawkers were scattering everywhere, yelling and firing in all directions.

Jenny rose in the stirrups and rode toward a Jayhawker who had slowed his horse. Her rifle cracked. The Jayhawker fell backward from the saddle.

A flash of lightning showed another Jayhawker riding toward her.

Jessie yelled, "Jenny, watch out! There's one on your left!"

As the Jayhawker fired, Jenny bent low and kicked her horse into a run. The bullet ripped through the brim of her hat.

Jessie fired his rifle. The Jayhawker cursed, grabbing his leg. He fired twice at Jessie, who yelled as a bolt of lightning struck nearby.

Jessie's horse reared, throwing him. As the wounded Jayhawker moved in for the kill, Windham appeared on his pinto. The Jayhawker turned his horse to meet

Windham's charge. Before he could fire, a blast from Windham's Colt had knocked him from the saddle.

Jessie staggered to his feet, dazed, while drops of water splashed against his face. Windham rode over to him.

"Jessie, you hurt?"

"No, I'm not hit. The lightning spooked my horse."

"Get on behind me!" Windham yelled. "Hurry!"

Nearby, Stick and another Jayhawker had emptied their guns at each other. They fought from horseback, hand to hand, tumbling off into the grass.

The thunder grew louder, the rain heavier. With Windham's help, Jessie climbed on.

"Look!" Jessie yelled. "Stick's in trouble."

Stick was on top of the Jayhawker, holding him down, while another Jayhawker rode toward them, his pistol cocked.

"Hold on!" Windham told Jessie. "Hold on tight!"

Windham rode straight toward the Jayhawker, then nudged his pony into a quick right turn. The Jayhawker fired at Windham, missing badly.

Windham turned his horse back toward the Jayhawker, whose horse shied, throwing him off balance. Windham rode past, firing almost point-blank into the Jayhawker's chest.

Turning his pinto around, Windham found Stick mounting his roan. The sky had opened up and rain was pouring.

"Stick, you alright?" Windham asked.

"I'm good. I think we got most of them. Some of them hightailed it out of here."

"Have you seen Jenny?"

Stick pointed through the darkness. "Over there. Not too long ago. I saw her shooting."

Jessie called to her from the back of Windham's horse. "I don't hear her answering," Jessie said. "I hope nothing happened to her."

"She can't hear you in this rain," Windham told him.

"We've got to find her." Jessie's voice was tense. "I've got a bad feeling, a real bad feeling."

Thirty-five

JUDD BARRETT rode through the crossing back toward the cabin. His pistol was empty and he had no time to reload. He had to do something; Frank Windham had found them.

He had watched Windham and the others with him cut down the Jacobs bunch. He didn't see who all had fallen, but he knew those left alive had likely ridden off.

None of that mattered now. Everything was ruined. Frank Windham had done that.

Barrett had decided he had one whole card left to play. There was one sure way to get to Windham, and that was through the women.

Barrett rode toward the corrals. The rain began to let up. Most of the flames had already been choked out. He would go to the cabin, where Coly had the women, and he would wait for Windham to come looking for them.

The area around the corrals was black and smoldering, the ground hissing with the falling rain. Barrett found Coly standing by himself, holding his knife, his head down.

"Don't be mad at me, Judd. Please don't."

Coly's lower stomach was bleeding badly and there was a wound in his right shoulder.

"What the hell happened here?" Barrett asked, jumping down from his horse.

"One of them women, that young one, shot me," Coly managed. He was sniffling like a schoolboy.

"Where'd she get the gun?"

"It must have been Woods'," Coly slobbered. "I don't know. Please don't be mad at me, Judd. Please."

"How'd you get stabbed?"

"Please don't be mad, Judd. Please."

"Them women cut you?"

"I fell on it when she shot me. I hate her, Judd."

"How did you have so much trouble with them?" Barrett asked. "It shouldn't have been that hard."

Barrett suspected that Coly had been too bloodhungry to do what he had been told. But there was no use discussing it now.

Barrett looked around. "Where's the women now?"

"They run off," Coly replied. "But one of Jacobs' men caught them. I seen him taking them to the cabin."

"Why are you here?" Barrett asked. "Why didn't you go to the cabin, too?"

"I figured you'd be mad at me," Coly said. "I wanted to wait and tell you."

"Can you walk?" Barrett asked him.

"Not too good."

Barrett shoved Coly into the saddle. Coly squealed with pain. His hat kept falling off and Barrett got it for him twice, then left it on the ground.

"I want my hat, Judd."

"We'll get it later, Coly. I want to check on those women."

At the cabin, Barrett found that June and Karlie were being watched by one of Jacobs' men. They were both tied tightly.

"I found them hiding in the grass," the Jayhawker said. "I saw them running away from that little man there."

"You saw what happened?" Barrett asked him.

The Jayhawker pointed to Coly. "He wanted to knife these two women. Crazy. He was supposed to watch them for us. He didn't. Lucky I came along, or they'd be gone."

"Where's your boss?" Barrett asked.

"Out fighting them others, near as I can tell," the Jayhawker replied. "What are you doing here?"

"I came back to check on the women," Barrett said. "I've got a stake in them."

"Well, you about lost them." He pointed to Coly again. "That man's got no brains."

"I don't want you talking that way about him," Barrett warned. "You understand?"

"Well, I plan to tell Jacobs about this when he gets back here," the Jayhawker said. "He'll fight them others off and he'll be here wanting these women. I'll tell him what happened. He won't like it one bit."

"I don't think you'll be seeing Jacobs again," Barrett said.

"Why not?"

"Because he's gone, for one thing. And for another"—Barrett pulled his pistol and fired into the man's stomach—"you won't be alive anyway."

The Jayhawker doubled over and fell to the floor, gasping. Coly smiled, holding his stomach wound. He reached for his knife.

"Let me finish him, Judd. Let me."

"You sit down there and stay put," Barrett said. "When this is over, I'll find you a doc."

Barrett cocked his pistol again. The Jayhawker whined and put his hand out, as if to ward off the bullets.

Barrett emptied his gun. Fingers flew from the Jayhawker's hand. His head snapped back as a bullet slammed into his forehead. He flopped onto the floor, kicking.

June had turned her head away. Karlie watched. When it was over, she told Barrett, "You'd better just go while you can. You won't live through this."

Barrett was hauling the Jayhawker's body out. He dumped it alongside the cabin and looked up at the widow.

"You've had a strange bunch of visitors, haven't you?"

The widow had turned away from him, rocking, silent, looking into the east, where the light was breaking.

Barrett walked back inside. Karlie began warning Barrett again. "Your days are numbered, mister. I'd say this is your last day."

"We'll be just fine, me and Coly here," Barrett said. "But now you, and that mother of yours, that's another story."

Barrett walked over and grabbed Karlie by the hair.

"What are you doing?" she yelled. "Let go of me!"

June's eyes widened. "You leave her be. Jacobs will have your hide!"

"To hell with Jacobs," Barrett said. "He rode out of here. He lost his men to Windham and the others and he hightailed it. I don't aim to lose to Windham."

Barrett pulled Karlie to her feet by the hair. He

dragged her outside, past the widow rocking in her chair, and around the cabin.

"What are you doing?" Karlie gasped.

Barrett pulled his gun and put the barrel in Karlie's ear.

"Now, I want you to scream real loud," he said.

"What?"

"You heard me. I want you to scream as loud as you can. If you don't, I'll blow your head off. Understand?"

Karlie screamed.

"That's good," Barrett said. "Again."

Karlie screamed louder and longer.

"That's real good," Barrett said. "Now, we'll go back inside and wait. I think we'll have a visitor soon."

Thirty-six

THE RAIN had nearly stopped. The clouds were breaking up, and in the east, a faint gray light appeared.

Windham and Stick rode a ways apart, still looking for Jenny. Jessie was yelling for her, becoming more and more anxious.

"Take it easy, Jessie," Windham said. "We'll find her."

"It's not that I'm worried about finding her," Jessie said. "I just want her to be alive."

Stick yelled from nearby, "Here she is, over here."

Windham rode over and Jessie jumped off before the pony had stopped.

"Jenny! Are you shot? What's the matter?"

"I'll make it, Jessie," she said. "They got me in the leg is all."

"Can you get up?" Jessie asked.

"It's bleeding," Jenny explained. "I have to plug the wound with my finger."

Stick was kneeling beside her. "It's still too dark to see how bad it is."

From the distance came a woman's screams.

Jenny sat up. "Oh, God!"

The screams came again.

"That's Karlie!" Jenny said. She tried to rise, but the pain was too great. "Leave me and go find her. I know that's her!"

"I'll go," Windham said to Stick. "You watch her. I'll be back."

"I'll go with you," Jessie said.

"You have to listen to me this time, Jessie. You've been lucky so far. You can't go this time."

"You can't go after them alone."

"I'm not worried about how many there are," Windham said. "I think we got most everyone. I believe Barrett is with June and Karlie. He's likely expecting me. I can't keep him waiting."

Windham rode his pinto through the crossing. The dawn light was growing, smoke filtering up into the sky.

As he neared the cabin, Windham dismounted and left his pinto with the reins down. He studied the area, the smoldering corrals, the charred body in the grass. A lot had happened here.

Near the cabin, sitting in a rocker, was an old woman. Windham studied her closely. She smiled at him and began to sing.

"She sounds a bit strange, don't she?"

Windham turned and saw that the voice belonged to a large man with very hard eyes. He was forcing a young woman along beside him, holding her by the hair. He pushed her to her knees, holding a pistol at her head.

"Judd Barrett?" Windham asked.

"Good guess," Barrett said. "You can toss that Colt over here. Do it now!"

Windham flipped the gun toward Barrett, far enough out of his reach so that he wouldn't pick it up.

"So, you're Frank Windham. We finally get to meet. I've been waiting for this a long time."

"I should have guessed it was you when I saw the grave. I figured you'd buried your brother again."

"What?" Barrett said. His face was contorted in anger and confusion. "What are you talking about?"

"You keep burying your brother over and over," Windham continued. "He shouldn't have been a thief."

Barrett's breath quickened. "He was twice the man you'll ever be, Windham. He had a cause, like I do. We hate Rebels."

"The war's over, Barrett."

"No, it won't ever be over," Barrett argued. "There'll be another Rebel cause, you wait and see."

Windham studied Barrett, thinking of an angle to work the man's anger against his other emotions, disturbing the plan he had set in his mind. If he could get Barrett to feel rage and sorrow at the same time, Barrett might forget what he had wanted to do.

Inside, June was watching Coly. She felt like screaming, herself. She was certain that Coly was going to kill her.

Coly was dying and he knew it. He held his stomach with one hand and toyed with his knife in the other. He stared at her, a strange smile working at the corners of his mouth.

"Where's your willow, Coly?" June asked. "Did you lose it?"

Coly's expression changed. He looked around, realizing he had lost it. He sat back against the wall, brooding.

June drew a deep breath. Maybe he wouldn't think about killing her again for a while. She could only hope, while she listened to the conversation outside and prayed that Karlie would live.

Barrett had started to ramble in his speech. Windham stood in front of him, listening as he defended his dead brother.

"Kelly was as good as they come," Barrett was saying. "He could fight, he could. He could soldier and whore with anybody. Because of you, he's gone. Now I'm going to settle things with you."

"So, let the women go," Windham said, taking a step forward. "This is between you and me."

"No, I want you to see her die. You've come a long ways. I know you figured on saving them. I want you to see this."

Windham took two more steps toward Barrett. Barrett turned the pistol away from Karlie's head and trained it on Windham.

"You stand back, you hear? I don't want you no closer."

"Shoot me, then," Windham said. "I don't think you can." Windham took another step.

Barrett brought the pistol back to Karlie's head. "You come any closer and I'll shoot her right now," Barrett said.

"Sure. She's something you can hit, isn't she? Are you sure you won't miss from there?" He took another step.

"Back up!" Barrett warned. He turned the pistol back on Windham.

"You're no different than your brother," Windham

told him, holding his ground. "You've got to have something to hide behind."

Barrett set his jaw. "Watch what you say about my brother."

"You mean that scumbag bluebelly, who couldn't soldier or whore? Isn't he the one that wore a dress? Yeah, he was wearing a dress the day I shot him."

Barrett was glaring at Windham, his breath ragged, giving Karlie a chance to turn and bite his wrist.

Barrett yelled and released his grip on her hair. Karlie scrambled off to the side, giving Windham the chance to rush in.

Windham had Barrett's arm in the air as the pistol went off. Windham brought the arm down across his knee. The bone cracked like dry wood.

Barrett yelled. Windham slammed a fist into his face. Barrett staggered. Again Windham hit him. Barrett fell backward over Duncan's body, struggling to keep his feet, then fell through the door into the cabin.

As Barrett rose again, Windham landed his fist into the man's midsection. Barrett grunted and grabbed Windham with his good arm, head-butting him.

Windham fell back against the doorsill. Barrett lunged at him, slamming his fist into Windham's head and neck. Windham slid down and out from under Barrett, swinging his fist into Barrett's kidneys.

Barrett groaned. Windham continued to hammer at his stomach and kidneys. Exhausted, Windham stopped for breath.

Barrett turned and grabbed Windham from behind in a bear hug. He was yelling against the pain in his arm, but his grip was locked.

As Windham struggled to free himself, Barrett slung

him sideways. Windham's head struck the wall and he slumped, dazed, in Barrett's arms.

June began yelling. Coly had struggled to his feet and was going toward Windham, gripping his knife tightly.

"Somebody stop him!" June yelled. "Please, somebody!"

June turned away, unable to watch, and passed out.

Thirty-seven

BARRETT HELD Windham up while Coly came ahead with the knife. He was babbling, licking his lips, staring at Windham's stomach.

Karlie came through the doorway, her hair matted, her eyes ablaze with anger. She was holding Windham's pistol.

"Coly, I've got something for you."

Coly stopped and stared vacantly. He started for Windham again.

Karlie fired. The round struck Coly full in the chest, knocking him backward against the table. He dropped the knife. She fired again, and again. Coly's eyes rolled and he fell heavily to the floor, sprawling among the spilled vegetables.

Barrett was yelling in rage. He released Windham and slammed a fist into the side of Karlie's head. Windham blocked a second blow as Karlie sagged to the floor, dropping the pistol.

Windham sent his right fist into Barrett's nose. His face covered with blood, Barrett staggered back toward the table, catching himself against the wall.

He looked down at Coly's body, roared loudly, and picked up the knife, charging Windham with all his might.

Windham had recovered his Colt. He emptied the remaining three shots into Barrett. The big man bounced from the wall to the floor, falling over Coly. He arched his back, let out a huge rush of air, and lay still.

Stick and Jenny came in the doorway. Jenny's leg was bandaged. The wound wasn't serious.

Karlie came to her feet. "Jenny? Is it really you?"

Jenny, standing on one leg, leaning back against the doorframe, hugged Karlie tightly. They fell to the floor and rolled, laughing and crying at the same time.

Jessie was untying June, trying to hug her while he worked at her bonds.

"Untie her first," Stick said. "You've got plenty of time to say hello."

Windham reloaded quickly and stepped out the door. The clouds had lifted and the sun was fully risen, filling the plains with light. The widow was smiling, rocking quietly.

The corrals and grasslands smoldered. Scattered on both sides of the crossing were horses, grazing peacefully.

From the east came two riders. They stopped at the hill overlooking the cabin. Windham laughed and waved them down.

Slack Cardwell and Jake Malone rode up to Windham and dismounted.

"What are you doing here?" Cardwell asked, slapping Windham on the shoulder.

"I was about to ask you two the same thing," Windham said.

"The herd is about a day east of here," Cardwell said. "We saw the smoke and decided to check it out. I was afraid a big range fire would force us to turn the herd."

"Lucky for the storm," Windham said. "That might have happened."

"We've been lucky all the way around," Jake Malone put in. "Charlie Graham's doing real good. Since you've left, it's been a picnic. No trouble of any kind."

"By the looks of things, you didn't have no picnic here," Cardwell said.

"No picnic," Windham agreed. "But I told you I'd get those horses back."

"We can use them." Cardwell smiled.

The others came out of the cabin. June and Karlie were on both sides of Jenny, supporting her. She insisted on standing by herself.

Jessie was holding his rifle, looking hard at Cardwell and Malone.

"These are some of the men that Stick and I work with," Windham said. "They came to help us drive the horses back."

Stick was smiling. "Yeah, they got here just in time."

"What's so funny?" Cardwell asked. "I didn't say I'd hire you back."

"I didn't say I'd come back." Stick laughed. "I have to say, this will be the first time ever that I've looked forward to seeing a bunch of mangy beeves. They'll look right pretty to me, I'm afraid."

"Well, Stick, most of them are prettier than you," Cardwell said. "But I guess they're prettier than any of us."

Malone was watching Jenny and Karlie. "I would say there are some exceptions to that."

"I wouldn't get on the bad side of either of them," Windham said. He talked about how well everyone had worked together. "Especially this young gun," he said, slapping Jessie on the back. "We couldn't have made it without him."

"I say we give him a couple of horses," Stick suggested. "And maybe a couple for Jenny, too."

Cardwell agreed. Jessie mounted his horse and told Jenny he would pick two for her. Stick rode with him while Cardwell and Malone began rounding up the herd.

Karlie thanked Windham. "I can't tell you how much I appreciate what you've done for all of us," she said. "You've been good to Jenny and Jessie."

"Those two can handle themselves," Windham said. He turned to Jenny. "What do you plan to do now?"

"We'll start over, Jessie and I," she said. "We'll go back with June and Karlie. We'll do fine." She looked out to where they were rounding up horses. "I figure you'll do fine, too. But if you ever get back this way . . ."

Windham wanted to take her in his arms. Instead, he took a step toward his horse. "It would be good to stay, Jenny. But . . ."

"I know," Jenny told him. "You don't have to explain."

Jessie returned, beaming with pride, leading four horses. Stick rode up next to him and shook his hand.

"I'll miss you, Jessie. You take care of your sister and your kin."

Jessie blinked away a tear. "I won't forget you, or Mr. Windham."

Windham was on his horse. He rode over and shook

Jessie's hand, also. "You'll do well," he said. "Keep practicing the Indian ways that I showed you."

"You didn't show me nearly enough," Jessie said. "Will you come back sometime and show me more?"

"I'd like to, Jessie. Who can say? Maybe."

Windham and Stick rode up to meet Cardwell and Malone, who were sitting their horses on the hill. They waved a last time and began to drive the remuda back toward the herd.

Windham took a last look down toward the cabin. Jenny was still waving, her long hair blowing in the morning breeze.

As he rode away, he hoped their lives would settle into peaceful times, and that the big plains would give them good grass and water. No one deserved it more than they, or June and Karlie.

Ahead, Cardwell and Malone were whistling at the horses, keeping them moving. Stick was riding at a gallop, looking into the morning sun.

The thunder had moved to the east, where a morning rain was falling. In every direction lay a vast, unending open, the only life Frank Windham could ever know.

Turn the page for a preview of

the next exciting Buffalo Brothers' adventure

COLORADO GOLD

Coming in January 1995 from Forge Books

An imprint of Tom Doherty Associates, Inc.

ISBN 0-812-53402-6

(Forge logo)

THE MIDDAY sun shone like fire through a wind-swept sky. The air was filled with sand blown like shards of glass across the open plains.

A lone horseman on a stout buckskin rode with his bandanna protecting his face and his hat low over his eyes. Joel McCann had been in the saddle for over twenty-four hours. He cared little about the sand and heat. He had a destination, and he would stay on his horse until he reached it.

McCann had just crossed the Texas border, into New Mexico Territory. He rode on until he could see a grove of paloverde, waving like large shadows in the wind and dust.

He had reached the Cimarron River. He knew that a few adobe buildings stood among the trees, the only settlement for miles in any direction.

The tiny village of Carminga lay along the Cimarron

Cutoff, a shortcut along the Santa Fe Trail. In years past, the trail had been used by fur traders moving in and out of Taos. Now it was just a quicker way to reach the growing Southwest, or travel on into California.

The road was shorter, but the chances of dying from thirst or thieves was much greater. For McCann, it was his journey's end, the place where he was to meet an old friend.

McCann was already three days late in reaching Carminga. He hoped Corky Devlin had not given up hope.

Coming down from Colorado, the telegraph from Devlin had said. *Will meet you on 1 May in Carminga where we spoke in the small saloon two years past. Will save the details for then. You won't be disappointed at the news I bring.*

McCann had gotten the telegraph in Fort Worth, where he spent what little time he wasn't in the saddle. Corky Devlin was someone Joel McCann could not disappoint. They had fought together during the Southern rebellion, in what folks were now calling the Civil War.

Though Devlin was unpredictable at best, McCann looked upon him as more than a brother. Devlin had saved his life during the last battle at Bull Run. McCann had fallen and Devlin had stood over him and kept the onslaught of blue from overrunning them.

Despite his wounds, McCann had gotten to his feet and had continued to fight.

"You'd best sit yourself down, lad, and save what strength you've got," Devlin had insisted. "You're no help, you know, and I've got more to do than save your butt all the day long!"

Devlin had saved his life not just once that day, but three times.

Four years had passed since the end of the war.

McCann had spent the entire time trying to forget what he had seen and felt, and what he had lost.

He had not wanted to join the Confederacy but had been told it was either wear the colors or go to prison for stealing cattle. Though he had stolen no livestock from anyone, he had marched into battle.

This had come less than a year into his marriage to Minnie Storm, a childhood sweetheart. He had also left behind his ten-month-old son, Clint.

Now every mile he rode and every town he came to he thought about them. He had returned from the war to find them gone—taken, it was said, by thieves.

Joel McCann spent every spare moment searching. He would never stop until he found his wife and son, dead or alive. He needed to know, one way or another.

McCann now hoped that the telegraph had something to do with his lost family. Had Devlin met them somewhere? He had shown Devlin their photographs many times during the war. Maybe Devlin had found them settled somewhere in Colorado Territory. A thousand possibilities ran through his mind.

As he neared the edge of town, McCann pulled his Colt Navy .44 and spun the cylinder. He also made certain that the action on his Henry rifle worked smoothly.

The war had not been good to him, nor had the years since. He had fought to save himself many times. He had learned to be cautious, no matter how peaceful his surroundings looked.

Carminga lay dormant, except for three horses tied in front of the lone saloon, called the Mockingbird. A small boardinghouse sat nearby, seemingly vacant, as was the livery stable just beyond.

McCann dismounted and led his buckskin to a watering trough at one of the hitching posts. The trees offered welcome shelter against the wind, the only shelter McCann had found in his two full days of riding.

McCann dusted himself off with his hat and stepped into the saloon. The inside was dark and smelled of smoke and spilled whiskey. In one corner, near a small window, was a barber pole.

An old man lay sleeping under a table near the pole, snoring loudly. Three men played cards along one wall. They looked up from their game and stared.

A bartender stood, polishing glasses. He was small and stooped over, in late middle age, with long side-burns and a thick, flowing mustache.

He turned and studied McCann. "Help you?"

"Let's start with whiskey and water back."

"Whatever you'd like." The bartender poured water into a coffee cup from a jug along the back bar. He filled a shot glass, then watched McCann down the whiskey and pour the water after it, smacking his lips. He set out the shot glass for another.

The bartender poured, his hands shaking. "Need a shave and haircut? I'll wake him up."

"Not today," McCann replied. "Maybe another time."

The bartender went back to polishing glasses. It was quiet, but for the wind outside and the barber's snoring. The three men at the table continued to stare.

"The town seems pretty empty," McCann remarked.

"Drying up," the bartender said. "Nobody will stay and run the boardinghouse and livery. I can't do it all myself."

"Maybe you should get some women," one of the men at the table said. "I've been wanting one for a while." The other two laughed.

"I tried that," the bartender said. "They don't stay on. They ride out with somebody first chance they get."

McCann studied the three men. Two of them looked

enough alike to be brothers. They wore similar hats and clothing and were light complected, well into their thirties, with slim faces and quick, darting eyes.

The third one, who wanted a woman, was large and dark, and younger than the brothers. He wore a battered Stetson, tipped back. He was rocking on his chair. His nose was hooked to one side and his heavy beard was filled with dust.

The bartender drew water from a pump at the end of the bar and filled a jug. He poured more water for McCann.

"It's a bad day for riding," he said. His hands were shaking. "It's the breath of hell itself out there."

"I'm here on purpose," McCann said.

The bartender laughed nervously. "That so. I figured you were lost."

"I'm looking for a man about this tall." McCann held his hand out at shoulder height. "His name's Devlin. Corky Devlin. He's about ten years older than me, built strong, and wears a red derby hat."

The bartender's eyes shifted to the three men at the table, and back to McCann. "A red derby?" His hands shook even more.

"Yeah. It might be a little dusty, but it's red. You wouldn't mistake it."

The three men at the table began whispering. The bartender looked toward them and went back to wiping glasses, but his hands shook so violently that, after dropping two, he gave up.

"He should have come in here a couple or three days back," McCann said. "I don't know. Maybe he's not gotten here yet."

"Haven't seen nobody like that," the bartender said. "Nobody in a red derby. You're right, he must not have come yet." His eyes again went to the three at the table.

McCann turned to the table. "How about it? Any of you seen someone who fits that description?"

The big one turned from his cards. He smiled at McCann, exposing a large gap in his teeth. "Nobody in a red hat would stay in here for very long. I wouldn't let him." He laughed.

The other two snickered. One of the brothers, older and slightly larger, looked up quickly to see McCann, leaning back with his elbows on the bar, staring hard at the big man.

"You say you don't like red hats?" McCann asked.

"Leon was just funning you, that's all," the brother told McCann. "Weren't you, Leon?"

"He's right. I don't like red hats," the big man said. "I won't let anybody stay here if they wear red hats. That's the way it is."

"You know something," McCann told the big man, "this hat I'm wearing, it used to be red. It used to be bright red."

The big man laughed. "No, that's not a red hat."

"Sure it is," McCann said. "Are you blind?"

The big man's smile disappeared. "What did you say?"

"I told you that I wear red hats," McCann said, still leaning back. "If this one doesn't look red to you, then you're blind."

The big man slid his chair back. The bartender retreated to the far end of the bar. The older brother leaned over toward the big man.

"Don't. There's another way."

McCann eased off the bar, his arms falling loosely at his sides, his right hand near the butt of his Colt. "Yeah, I'm sure of it. I'd have to say you're blind. And stupid to boot."

The two brothers stood up quickly. "Leon, it's time to go," the older brother said. "I already told you that."

The big man stood up and shook them off. "No. I've got business with this red hat man first."

"We don't need any shooting, Leon," the younger brother said. "Say good-bye to the stranger and we'll be on our way."

"I can take him."

McCann was watching the other two as closely as he watched the big man. Neither of them seemed to be anxious to fight, but you never knew.

"I'm going to take him," the big man repeated.

"Forget it, Leon," the older brother demanded. "Let's go."

"You two go. I'll come later."

"Leon, we'll come back another time."

"Yeah," the younger brother said. "We'll come back again. Soon."

"I'm not ready to go yet."

"Leon, you aren't listening," the older brother insisted.

The big man studied the brothers. "Oh, I see." He was smiling. "Yes, we'll go." He started for the door behind the brothers. "Enjoy your stay, red hat man. I'll be seeing you again some time."

"Maybe," McCann said.

As soon as the three had left the saloon, McCann pulled his Colt and turned the table sideways, spilling the cards and chips onto the floor. He took cover behind it.

The bartender was crouched behind the bar, trembling. Outside, the wind whined. Inside, the old barber snored and McCann cocked his pistol.

The three burst into the saloon, shooting wildly. The big man and the older brother were in front. McCann fired two shots into the older brother, knocking him backward. He fell over the sleeping barber, who raised his head momentarily.

The older brother crawled along the floor and sat up against the wall, holding his chest, looking around with a dazed expression. The younger brother slid behind the bar, while the big man sprayed bullets into the table where McCann was crouched, yelling, "I'll kill you, red hat man! I'll kill you!"

Wood splinters flew everywhere. McCann rolled away, a bullet grazing his right shoulder. He came to one knee and fanned his Colt. Bullets slammed into the big man, turning him in a half circle.

He fell sideways into the bar. The pistol in his left hand discharged and fell to the floor. The big man caught himself, holding his heavy body up with his left elbow, and turned around.

McCann talked from behind the table. "You had enough?" he asked the big man, watching for the younger brother to come up over the bar.

The big man stared at his chest. Blood was staining the front of his shirt. He slowly raised his remaining pistol. "Red hat man. I'm going to . . . shoot you."

McCann aimed over the table and fired. The bullet slammed into the big man's forehead. He dropped like a huge sack of flour, thudding heavily to the floor.

Gunfire came from over the bar, splintering the table and nearby chairs. McCann ducked behind another table and reloaded quickly. He heard the younger brother's boots as he ran from the saloon. Soon he was kicking his horse into a dead run out of town.

The older brother, still seated against the wall, began to laugh.

McCann stood up. The room was filled with smoke and the smell of death. He approached the older brother cautiously, while the man stared at him and continued to laugh.

"You see this as funny?" McCann asked him.

He coughed and wiped blood from his mouth. "I can't cry."

"Who are you?"

"It doesn't matter now. I'm dead."

"You make bad choices, sooner or later it'll catch up with you."

"Save your religion speech."

"What's this all about?" McCann asked.

The man ignored him. He was shaking his head. "I knew we should've waited." His face twisted into a frown. "Any other time would've been better. That stupid DuCain!" He coughed again. "Now look . . . look at what's happened." His chin dropped and he fell sideways, air escaping from his lungs.

The bartender came out from behind the bar and stared at the bodies.

"You're a deadly man."

"I've got some questions for you, mister," McCann said. He walked toward the bartender, his pistol still drawn, but pointed toward the floor.

The bartender raised his hands. "Don't shoot. Please! I had no part in it. I swear!"

"Did you know any of these men?"

"Not any of them. I swear. They came in yesterday. I didn't know them, I swear."

"You've seen Corky Devlin, the man in the red derby, though, haven't you? I could tell by the way you acted. You and these men knew who I was talking about, didn't you?"

"Yes, but I had no part in it. I swear!"

"No part in what? What are you talking about?"

"Listen, they told me they'd cut me in on the deal. If

I just went along with them, I'd get a share. But I told them I didn't want no part of it."

"What are you talking about?"

"The gold. They talked about the gold."

"What gold? Make some sense, bartender. What are you talking about?"

"Listen, maybe you should talk to your friend." The bartender pointed to the back door. "There's a shed behind. Your friend's in there. The red derby man's in there."

"Back there? In a shed? Why?"

"They put him in there," the bartender said. "Please, just let me go."

McCann squinted at him. "What are you afraid of?"

"I just figured those men would kill me," the bartender said. "Now I figure you will. I don't want to die."

McCann pointed. "Hand me that jug of water."

The bartender hurried behind the bar. He struggled, his hands shaking violently. McCann reached out and grabbed the jug.

The bartender pointed toward the back. "He's in the shed. You'll find him easy enough."

"You'll take me back there," McCann insisted. "I don't want to have to use my gun again."

"No, no. You won't have to. You won't. I'll take you."

The bartender led the way out the back door, turning his head often to see if McCann was preparing to shoot him. McCann, who had holstered his Colt, became increasingly disgusted.

"You're lucky I don't wring your neck, mister."

"Nothing against you, I swear," the bartender said. "But those three, they would've killed me sure."

"How could you think they'd make a deal with you, for gold or anything else?"

"I just don't want to die, mister. That's all."

The bartender opened the door to a small adobe shed and pointed inside. As McCann peered in, the bartender began running through the alley.

McCann let him go and stepped into the shed. On the floor sat Corky Devlin, bound and gagged, wearing his famous red derby. His eyes widened.

McCann pulled the gag free and began to untie him. "I didn't expect this, Corky. Fine way to spend an afternoon."

Devlin wiped his brow and reached for the water. "Damn, it's hot! And that wind. Did you ever see the likes of it?" He drank greedily, until McCann slowed him down.

"Not too fast, Corky. There's plenty of water and plenty of time now."

"I'm beholden to you, Joel. I'm about cooked, I am."

"Would you like to tell me about this?" McCann asked.

Devlin noticed the crease along the top of McCann's shoulder. "I heard the shooting. I wasn't worried about you, though, Joel. Not a-tall. You're one for getting in and out of scrapes, you are. . . . Of course, I've helped on occasion. You'll grant me that."

"Granted. Now you'll consider this as a payback."

"You'll get no argument from me. I've saved you three times, though. You've got two left."

"Let's not rush things," McCann said. "How did you get into all this in the first place?"

"By sending you the wire," Devlin replied. "That's how it all began. I told the man operating the telegraph about our good fortune, and he must have told Mr.

Hurlan. Then Mr. Hurlan, fiend that he is, sent those three after me."

"Mr. Hurlan?"

Devlin gulped more water. "Marvin Hurlan. He wants our gold!"

"Our gold?"

"That's what I wired you about, Joel. Yes, we're rich, we are. You and me, lad. We've got gold in the Colorado Rockies. A great mountain of gold, lad!"

McCann frowned. "Are you talking about that claim we put in together ten years back? That's hardly worth all this."

"The very same one. And it is worth all this."

"I thought you told me during the war that the claim was a bust."

"Ah, but it was then. Times have changed, Joel. Times have changed. True, there wasn't much surface gold where we had our claim, but I'll tell you, there's a lode underground, a mother lode at that."

"I don't know anything about underground mining," McCann said. "Nor do you."

"We can learn, lad," Devlin insisted. "There's new ways of getting the gold out of the rock. There's mills a-popping up like trees everywhere. A railroad's planned to come up from Denver."

"A railroad?" McCann said. "I didn't think that country would ever come alive again."

"It's true, the place died down for a good time," Devlin said. "But you'd ought to see it now. You'd really ought to see it now. That's why those three came after me."

"Tell me now, who's Marvin Hurlan?" McCann asked.

"He's a businessman in Central City who's investing in the new railroad," Devlin replied. "He came up from

Denver. Now he's looking for the good claims in the area. He'll do anything to take them. I guess I should've known he'd want ours to boot."

"So he sent hired killers after you," McCann said. "He didn't want you getting back to Central City?"

"He didn't want *either* of us getting back there, lad. You should know that by now. I rode the back trails, in case of someone followed me, but they were here waiting when I rode into town. The telegraph man must've told Hurlan everything."

"You must've told the telegraph man everything," McCann said. "Don't you know better than that?"

"Oh, but Joel, lad, I was so happy for the two of us, and nobody else to share it with. But you're right, I opened me mouth, and I'm sorry for that."

"I don't know why they didn't kill you right away," McCann said. "I don't know why they bothered to tie you up."

"Because I lied to them, Joel," Devlin said. "I told them you had a map to another diggings, and that we were planning on filing more claims. They wanted to learn about that, you see."

"What?"

"I had to tell them something, Joel. Otherwise they would've killed me sure. You just said it. They would have killed me right away. We couldn't have that, now could we? After all, we've got to mine that gold together."

"Two of them won't be killing anyone now."

"The two brothers," Devlin continued, "the Carltons, are the worst kind of killers. Hurlan uses them a lot. Folks in the diggings know about them."

"There's only one of them left," McCann told him. "I got one of the brothers and the big man."

"Leon DuCain. The big, dirty one. That's good to know. Which one of the brothers did you get?"

"The bigger one. He looked to be the older."

Devlin frowned. "Len Carlton. It would have been better to have gotten Lon, the little brother. That it would. But we can't be a-fretting over that, now can we?"

McCann went to the door. The wind was still blowing strongly. Devlin drank more water and began rubbing the circulation back into his hands and feet.

"They tied me up proper, they did. I'd like to do the same to them."

"There's only one left, Corky. Remember?"

"Ah, that's right. Thanks for reminding me. I'll sleep lots better, I will. Lon Carlton is worse than the other two combined, he is."

"I wonder where he went," McCann said. "And I don't trust that bartender."

"Ah! Don't worry none about that bartender. He's likely still running. Most spineless fiend I ever laid eyes on."

"They're the kind who'll shoot you in the back," McCann pointed out. "I'd like to rest a little, over in that boardinghouse, but I don't want him sneaking up on me."

"You'd fare better to worry about Lon Carlton," Devlin said. "But I'll keep an eye open while you rest. It's the least I can do for you." He rose to his feet and stumbled. "I feel a little faint."

"You drank too much water. Sit down a minute."

"I'll sit in the boardinghouse. I can't stand the likes of this shed any longer, nor this little town, for that matter. I'd never take holidays here, you can bet on that."

McCann helped Devlin to the door. "You picked this place. Why would you want to come all the way down

1ere? You could have told me the news in the telegram.
Tou told everyone else."

"I had another surprise for you, lad," Devlin said. "It
vas about your family, your wife and son."

"You found them?"

"Well, I had learned they were in this country. But I
:ouldn't be certain. I'm still not certain. You get your
'est and we'll travel on."

"I don't care much about resting now. I'd as soon
ook for my family."

"We can't go in this wind," Devlin remarked. "Be-
;ides, you need the rest. Your eyes are about puffed
.hut."

McCann helped Devlin through the back door and
nto the saloon. Flies were collecting on the bodies in
arge numbers. The barber lay on the floor, still asleep.

Devlin looked around and shook his head. "This
)lace is a mess. I'd say the bartender had best get to
work."

"I figure the younger brother will be back to bury his
<in," McCann said. "Maybe we can end our relationship
with him then."

Devlin slipped behind the bar and selected a couple
)f bottles. "It's even odds either way, I'd say. Lon Carlton looks after himself and cares about nothing or no
)ne else." He popped the cork on one and took a long
swallow. "If I was a betting man, I'd say you're right.
He'll be back. But I never bet. You know that, lad."

McCann started for the door. "I'm going to the boardinghouse. I'll get some rest. And we'll go."

Devlin grabbed a third bottle and stuck it under his
arm. He took another drink and stopped beside the
sleeping barber. "Maybe I'll wake him up later for a
shave."

"How about if I give you a shave?" McCann suggested. "I'll bet my hand is steadier."

"Ah, but you got me there, lad." He took one last look around the saloon and took a deep breath. "All this in the name of riches. 'Tis a pity, isn't it?" He winked at McCann. "Not to worry, though, lad. They're our riches, and we'll be using them for a good cause. Eh, lad? For a very good cause."